A Father's Justice!

John D. McCray

Olympus Story House

TABLE OF CONTENTS

Dedication

First and foremost, I would like to thank God for blessing me with my special talent to be able to write my ninth book. I would like to thank my mom and dad for always encouraging me to do my best in whatever I do in life. I would like to thank my siblings for always supporting me, Lamont, Brian, Shakelia, Tyra and Leana. I would also like to thank some special people that always gave me that extra push that I needed when I felt like giving up and has supported me from day one; Isiah Lemon, Erica Capers, Matthew Collins, Anitra Hammett, Sylinda F. Johnson, Angela Richburg, Lawanda Samuels, Kevina S. Mouzon, Sharia White, Tangie Armstrong, Rhonda Williams, Elroy Wilson, Ethel Barnett, Linda Smith, and Artrice N. Singleton. I would like to thank two great people who are no longer here and are looking down on me from above. Thank you both for your support through the years and you are definitely missed Lee Pickens, and Tyrone Fogle. Last but not least, I would like to thank my grandparents who are no longer here, the late John and Daisy Carraway and Richard and Ida Mae McCray. Thank you all for your love through the years. You are definitely appreciated.

CHAPTER 1

"Ryan Jacobs"

I just got home from work and dove straight in my bed. I bought a two-bedroom townhouse about five years ago but I'm thinking about getting a bigger place. I think I've outgrown this one but in order for me to get a bigger place, I'll need a bigger income. I'm a seventh grade Science teacher and right now my salary just isn't cutting it, besides dealing up with these bad, disrespectful kids. I didn't go through four years of college and two more years to obtain my Master's to deal with so many spoiled, know it all kids, telling me what they're going to do and not do.

When I think I'm making a difference in their lives, that's when I have to deal with their trifling parents, that barely have a seventh grade education themselves. I had one kid's father that wanted to fight me at the last PTA meeting we had because I simply told him that Wendell talks entirely too much in class and never turns in his homework or completes assignments. The father told me I was a liar and that if I didn't treat his son fairly, he was going to kick my gay behind.

I almost forgot that I was in a school setting, because I was about to tell Mr. Bennette to meet me outside so I could show him whose gay behind he was about to kick. This is the kind of thing I deal with at school and if it's not that, then its Ms. Smith, the school principal, dropping in to see how I'm conducting and teaching my class.

I wanted to tell Ms. Smith, if she feels like I'm not doing a good job or my teaching techniques aren't to her standards, maybe she should find someone else to teach my class. I'm just not that crazy to do that, especially since this job is how I pay my bills.

I felt my cell phone vibrating in my pocket. I took my phone out to see who was calling. It was Pickle, trying to setup a booty call tonight. Pickle's real name is Monteiro Gonzales but there's definitely a reason why I call him "Pickle", because he's definitely blessed and he knows it.

Pickle is half black and Puerto Rican, with a caramel mocha complexion. He's about six feet, and about one hundred and eighty pounds with solid muscles. Pickle is definitely easy on the eyes and has a slamming muscular body, showing off all his numerous tattoos when he wears his wife beater tee-shirts, whenever he comes over.

Pickle is a pretty cool guy but the one thing I don't particularly care about is that he's married. Pickle and Shontel have been together since they were kids and they have three children together. Pickle says he loves his wife and his kids but he just can't get me out of his system for him to be faithful to her.

I know one day I'll get a lot of this back on me for how I'm living my life. Sometimes to be honest, I don't know how I can stand to even look at myself in the mirror, knowing some of the things I've done and am still doing until this day, with breaking up people's homes. Shontel is my first cousin on my mother's side. Shontel's mother Edith and my mother were sisters.

Shontel and I have never been close but my Aunt Edith and I are. After my mom died when I was fifteen, in a terrible car accident, Aunt Edith took me under her wing and helped my father with me. It wasn't like she had to do much, since I was basically already grown but what she did meant the world to me and my father.

Shontel is Aunt Edith's oldest child but she has a son Anthony, that's my age and we're close like brothers. I know Shontel would be furious if she knew that Pickle and I have been messing around about five years now, since Aunt Edith's husband, Uncle Red died.

Shontel isn't right for Pickle and he complains about her all the time. Shontel has a mean, angry attitude that if you ask her how she's doing, she might bite your head off for even asking her. She's very nice looking and has a shape from out of this world but her personality is on a totally different level.

Shontel doesn't cook or clean their house but she stays shopping all the time. She loves her designer Louis Vuitton and her Michael Kors purses and the other name brands she wears. Shontel won't work in a pie factory but thinks she deserves all expensive things.

Pickle is a foreman for a construction company and he sells a little dope on the side as well. I guess Pickle sells drugs just to keep up with Shontel's lavish lifestyle, which is pathetic. I will say one thing about her, she makes sure their kids are dressed nice and her daughter's hair is always done.

I hung up the phone with Pickle and told him he could come over about nine o'clock tonight. I don't know why it's easy for Pickle to get out of the house like that on a weekday but I guess Shontel doesn't question him too much, since she knows what he does on the side and the allowance he gives her as well.

I shook my head, wondering why I can't find a man like that, that's not attached to anyone else, like my evil, ghetto behind cousin, Shontel. I would be good to him and treat him like a king but I guess since I haven't, I'll have to keep dealing with someone like Pickle forever.

I sat on my bed, looking at myself in the mirror on my wall. It's not my fault that I'm a little promiscuous and the way I am, since God made me to be handsome, with dark chocolate and blemish free skin, at 5'10, weighing one-hundred and sixty-five pounds. I've always kept a low faded hair-cut, which displayed my deep, dark waves, that I'm always brushing when I think about it. I definitely wouldn't leave out my sense of style by the way I dress. I would say that on a scale from one to ten, God made me a twelve, not to be tooting my own horn or anything but God did good.

God knew exactly what he was doing when he created me to be all this. I couldn't help from smiling at myself as I continued checking myself out, as if this was my first time looking in the mirror today. My looks don't define me to be a terrible or a conceited person because I know being that way would never get me anywhere in life.

My mom always said, "beauty is only skin deep, but the heart is what is pure but could hurt you to the core." I knew how hurt felt when I lost my mother in that car accident, or the way my Dad sometimes looks at me when he wished I was something that I'm not.

My father and I are extremely close now but it hasn't always been like that, and sometimes I think he's still a little disappointed in me that I'm gay but he seems to accept it a lot more now than he did when I was younger. If my dad ever found out some of the things I dealt with in my childhood, all hell would break loose and I can never let that happen.

CHAPTER 2
"Robert Jacobs"

I just pulled up to Olive Garden at eleven-forty. I'm supposed to have lunch with my two best friends that I grew up with, Myron Jenkins and Shelvin Johnson. All three of us are the same age and we just celebrated our fifty-first birthday three months ago at Ruth's Chris with our families.

I walked into Olive Garden and told the hostess that I was here to meet my two best friends. I gave the young lady my name and she took me to the table. "What's up boss man," Myron said, as he gave me a big bear hug like he always does. "Myron, it's good to see you again," I said, embracing my friend. "Good to see you to Rob. Isn't it good to be above the ground, instead of in the ground," Myron said, flashing that sneaky little white smile he always had growing up, that made all the ladies go crazy over him. "It certainly is," I replied, shaking my head at Myron.

"What's going on old man?" Shelvin said, hitting me on the arm, extending his arms out to hug me. "I got your old man Shelvin, since we're all the same age," I said, laughing. "Oh yeah, I forgot about that, but I look better and younger," Shelvin said, rubbing his chin with confidence. "I guess you did forget about that," I said, as we all sat down.

I don't get to hang out with my boys too much since we all have busy lives and schedules but when time permits, we do get to meet up from time to time to at least have a drink and shoot the breeze over some fishing from time to time. I guess we all need to unwind a little and tell each other how our week and personal lives are going.

Myron is an engineer for McIntosh and has been there for twenty-eight years, and Shelvin is an architect that just opened up his own business about two years ago. Myron is now divorced and has a twenty-seven-year-old son, MJ that lives in Atlanta. Shelvin has never been married but he has two grown children from an old girlfriend he dated right after college.

We all graduated from Benedict College in Columbia, South Carolina and pledged Phi Beta Sigma. I'm surprised that these two are single, especially how big of whores they were in high school and college. They were always running behind some hot tail girl in school, and plenty of times we all had to help each other fight their big brothers or boyfriends that the girls had but never told us about. I stayed getting my ass beat fighting for one of them.

I was never really like these two in college. Maybe I was just as bad as they were in high school but our sophomore year in college is when I started to change when I met Alexandria Ragin. Alexandria was the most beautiful, amazing, intelligent woman that I've ever met in my entire life.

Alexandria and I had our entire lives mapped out after a few months of dating. We were both going to become doctors and start our own practice. Things didn't exactly turn out like that for us though. Alexandria ended up getting pregnant with Ryan our junior year and had to put school on hold until she had our son. We ended up getting married at twenty-one and three months later, we became parents.

My parents were furious with me and they both accused Alexandria of messing up my life. Alexandria's family felt the same way about me, that I was trying to ruin her life, even though they hated what we had done, they still helped us out as much as they could.

I finished college with a degree in business and Alexandria went back after she had Ryan and finished with a nursing degree. We struggled a bit at first but after we got more established with good paying jobs, things quickly turned around for us.

I was so caught up traveling down memory lane, that I didn't hear the young lady. Shelvin nudged me on the arm, as I jumped. "What?" I asked, stretching my eyes. "You didn't hear the young lady asking you what you wanted to drink?" Shelvin said. "Oh no I didn't," I replied. "I'm sorry. What were you asking me?" I asked. "It's okay. I was asking you what would you like to drink?" the young lady asked. "I'll take a cup of water please," I said. "Sure thing," the lady said, as she left.

Myron started laughing out loudly. "Dang Rob, what were you thinking about to have you in deep thought like that? I know you weren't looking at our waitress like that because she's definitely no Halle Berry," Myron said, laughing. "No she's not but I was just thinking about our lives from when we were kids to high school and then our college years.

We've all been through some difficult times in our lives together. You know when Alexandria and I got married and when we found out that we were pregnant with Ryan. And when Ryan was a child and he had pneumonia, with all that fluid around his lungs and they thought he wasn't going to make it, and when I lost Alexandria in that car accident.

There were times I didn't know if I was going to make it. I depended on Alexandria for everything. I swear, you guys were there the entire time for me and Ryan. You all would keep Ryan at your house for a night or the weekend, when I didn't want Ryan to see me crying and grieving for his mother. I just want to say thank you both for always being there for me," I said.

I felt my eyes getting a little watery, like I was about to shed a few tears but I wouldn't allow them to fall. Not because I was embarrassed of anything, it was only because I needed to be strong and show them how much I appreciated them. "No problem man. That's what friends are for right?" Myron said. "That's right," I replied. "Man no matter what, we'll always have your back," Shelvin replied. "Yeah, I know," I said.

The waitress brought our drinks to the table and took our order. "How are things going with you and Airene," Shelvin asked. "I guess they're okay. Airene is definitely no Alexandria," I said. "You got that shit right," Myron said. "Man, I don't even know why you married her," Shelvin said, sucking his teeth.

Myron and Shelvin have never been fans of Airene. Airene is my second wife. We've been married for thirteen years and we have a twelve-year-old daughter named Robin. Airene has an older son Akeem, that lives with her ex-husband. Akeem tried staying with us for a while but I had to kick him out because he wasn't working and wasn't looking for a job, like someone was going to take care of his grown, nasty, twenty-three-year-old ass, like that.

Airene was upset when I made Akeem leave but I told her that every adult that's going to be living in our house is going to be working and helping contribute to the bills. I wasn't going to have another mouth to feed that could go out there and work for a living.

The waitress brought us our lunch and we continued talking and laughing and just catching up on our lives. Shelvin seemed like he was in a better place than the last time I saw him. His father died six months ago from brain cancer and Shelvin was so drunk out of his mind that night, that someone from the bar he was at called me and told me to come get him.

Myron and I came and got Shelvin from "Lucky Rounds" in Charlotte at two-o'clock that morning. Shelvin kept telling us he didn't need our help because he wasn't an alcoholic or anything. We didn't try to give him a lecture but we expressed our concerns to him and we would be there whenever he needed us to. A week later, Shelvin called and told us that demon of alcoholism had taken over his life and he needed our help and we were both there to help him make that first step down that road to recovery.

Shelvin looks good now, like he has his life back together. Myron is acting like he's on cloud nine, since his divorce and he's loving a care free life and being single right now. Shelvin and I both laughed and told him that every now and then that little snake wants to peek his head out and come out to play too. Myron joked and said, when he's ready, he lets him out. We both laughed at each other. I swear, there's nothing like laughter. It's definitely good for the soul.

CHAPTER 3
"Ryan"

I laid on top of my bed about to drift off, when a knock from my bedroom door made me jump. "Come in," I said. Jarod walked into my bedroom and sat on my bed. "What's up Ryan?" Jarod asked. "I'm good Jarod. Just a little tired but I'm okay," I said. "Rough day in class today?" Jarod asked. "Not really. Just the normal dealing with their disrespectful behinds," I said. "Oh I feel you on that," Jarod replied.

Jarod looked like he wanted to say something but didn't know how to say it. "Is there something you wanted?" I asked. "Yes. I might be a little late with my portion of the rent and bills this month," Jarod said. "Not this again Jarod. You've been late for the last three months. Just because you're going to be late, doesn't mean the bills aren't still due," I said. "You're right Ryan. I'll do better, "Jarod said. "You have to Jarod, because I can't keep paying your portion of the bills and be late on paying my own, because you won't do what you have to. It's rough on me to have to do that!" I said.

Jarod dropped his head as if he was a little child and was just scolded for something he did wrong. "I'm sorry Ryan. This will be the last time," Jarod said. "It better be Jarod, because this will be your last month living here if it happens again," I said. "Are you serious?" Jarod asked. "Yes I am. Paying your bills on time is a part of being an adult," I said. "You're right," Jarod said. "Okay, is there anything else?" I asked. "No, that's it," Jarod said, getting up from my bed and walking out of my bedroom.

Jarod and I have known each other for about ten years. We met in college when he came in on the first day, looking all confused to life and to the school. I asked him what building he was looking for and he said the engineering technology building.

I walked Jarod to the building and showed him to the counselor he needed to see. If I didn't think Jarod was cute, I would never have done that. He would've had to find the building the best way he could. Jarod was an engineering major but he couldn't handle all that different math he had to take so he changed his major to psychology.

Jarod is from a small town in South Carolina so when he came to UNC Charlotte to go to college, he was like a little hermit crab that was afraid to come out of his shell. My friends and I were able to bring Jarod completely out and I guess he's adapted well afterwards.

Jarod and I dated for about four months but I found out quickly in our relationship that we were totally opposite of each other, which I knew from the start but I think I was just ready to be with someone instead of being the only one in my social circle that was single.

I'm just glad that after Jarod and I knew it wasn't going to work in a relationship, we were able to remain friends. After graduation I told Jarod I had a job offer already lined up for me with a middle school that I went to as a child. I told him it was up to him if he was going to stay in Charlotte or come back to Gastonia with me, until he got more established. Jarod chose to room with me for a while, until he got in a relationship and moved out.

The guy Jarod started dating and eventually moved in with, was a piece of work. Floyd was his name and he was one of the biggest drug dealers around, with a terrible temper. One day after Jarod and Floyd got in a heated argument, Floyd jumped on Jarod and broke his nose and gave him a black eye. Jarod left him and came knocking on my door and me being the loyal good friend that I am, I opened up my door to him.

For some reason Floyd was like a drug to Jarod. It didn't matter how bad he mistreated him, Jarod always came back to him and I was always the one to be there to pick him back up. One particular day, Jarod came home from the weekend he spent with his parents and he found Floyd shot to death on their bedroom floor.

Jarod cried for weeks and weeks at a time grieving for Floyd, but he realized that Floyd wasn't coming back so he had to move on with his life. I talked with the principal at Ashbrook, Mr. Davison and asked him to help Jarod find a job at his school. Mr. Davison was definitely willing to help Jarod with getting the position but that wasn't all Mr. Davison wanted from Jarod.

Jarod eventually told me what Mr. Davison was doing to him. I showed Mr. Davison a picture that I had of him with a dog collar around his neck and him down on all four. I told him that I was going straight to Mrs. Davison as well as the school board. I'm happy to say that was the end of Mr. Davison harassing Jarod ever again.

Jarod always seemed to be getting himself into something and I'm always the one bailing him out of it and now it's him not paying his bills on time. I know I had to put my foot down on this one because Jarod was starting to make this a habit and I'm not having that. I told him this was going to be his last time. I have too much going on without dealing with him and his financial issues as well. I don't know why he's so broke because he makes more than I do and we both have Master's degrees. I hope he gets it together quickly for his sake.

I grabbed my things and went and took a quick shower. Pickle told me he'll be here around nine tonight, if his ghetto ass wife will let him out of the house. As the water hit my face, I thought about how I'm living my life and whether my mother would approve of it. I don't even have to ask that question because I already know the answer to it. I know my mother wouldn't and I could see her right now pointing her finger and telling me that I need to stop before something happens to me.

I've tried to live my life as discreet as possible and never trying to be a messy person or come off to anyone that I could be a threat, because that's how you get killed. In this line of work, you have to be on top of everything and know what you're doing as well as protect yourself at all costs. I won't let anyone burn me or think that just because I'm gay, that means I won't cut you or pull out my 9 mm on that ass because a brother definitely will.

I took the proper precautions to prepare myself for tonight, just to make sure I'm good. I sure hope Jarod won't be home but I'm sure he'll be right here. It's not like Jarod gets out like that anyway or knows many people like that. He told me he's been trying to meet people on the on-line dating apps, but he's a little scared with doing that. I told him he should be because there's some sick people out there that don't care anything about hurting anyone and I would hate to learn that anything has happened to him.

After Pickle comes over, he'll probably be here no longer than an hour tops, in order for him to do his thing and then go. I can't be mad at him because that's all I need him to do. I dried myself off and jumped on my website to set up two more appointments. Being an escort can make you some big money, especially all the connections you're introduced to as well.

Just for those two appointments, I'll make a thousand dollars in less than two and a half hours. I sure hope Pickle lays some cash on me just as well as he's laying the pipe, because Lord knows a brother needs everything I can get. With me covering all the rent until Jarod pays his portion of the bills, I pretty much have to do escorting to stay above water. I always knew how to hustle to make my bread by doing this as a result. I never thought I would ever have to prostitute my body just to get ahead but times are rough for everyone and I'm definitely no exception.

CHAPTER 4
"Robert"

Today was a pretty good day. I got the chance to have lunch with my two best friends and finished up two reports, that I'm sure the insurance companies will be very pleased with since the fire accidents weren't accidental and were actually arson.

I've been a fire inspector for almost thirty years and I can catch the ones that were done intentionally, from the ones that were actual accidents. Mr. Arnold Diaz owns "Pizza Italian Rolls," restaurant and mysteriously a fire broke out in the kitchen at about eleven-fifteen last night. When you first walk in the restaurant you can smell the gas over the smoke, as if someone mopped the entire floor in gas and then decided to light a match afterwards.

It's shocking to know the extremes that people will do to get some money. They will even burn down their house, car, and place of business and file that false claim. I don't think they realize that arson is a crime and they could go to prison for doing that. I hope things never get that bad for me that I ever have to result in doing that.

I grabbed the remote and started flipping through the channels on TV, trying to find something interesting to watch. "Hey baby," Airene said, as she walked towards me. "Hey baby," I said, embracing my wife and giving her a kiss on the lips. "How was your day?" I asked. "It was good. Nothing too exciting never happens in the public library, unless someone brings in a screaming child or a homeless person comes in there trying to have sex or whack it off in the corner, when they think no one is paying them any attention," Airene said.

I couldn't believe doing something like that in a public place, surrounded by children and other people that could possibly see them. I guess it's the thrill for them I suppose. "How was your day?" Airene asked. "It was good. I met Myron and Shelvin at Olive Garden for lunch," I said. "Oh," Airene said, frowning up her nose. "I sure hope you find some other friends to hang out with," Airene said. "Why you say that?" I asked. "Because you know they don't like me and they have some bad habits," Airene said. "How do you know what kind of habits they have when you're barely around them?" I asked.

Airene looked at me as if I should know she wasn't dumb or something. "Well for starters, neither one of them are married. No married man should be hanging around with single men like that, or less they still want the single life," Airene said. "Well, I don't hang around them like that. We barely get to see each other with how hectic our work schedules are." I said. "Well, maybe that's a good thing," Airene said.

I looked at Airene with a disgusted look on my face but didn't say anything. "And besides they both smoke weed and Shelvin is a recovering alcoholic. I'm just afraid you'll pick up some of their bad habits, Rob. That's all I'm saying," Airene said. "Look, please ease up off my friends like that. I don't talk about your friends or your family do I?" I said. "Well, I don't have any friends. I only have my two sisters, my children, and you. That's all I need," Airene said.

I just shook my head at Airene's comment because I can definitely see exactly why she doesn't have any friends, with an attitude like that. "Where's Robin?" I asked. "She's over at her friend's Tajah's house. She asked if she can spend the night and I told her she could," Airene said. "Hold up, doesn't Tajah's stepfather and her older two brothers live there too?" I asked. "Yes they do," Airene said, like it was no big deal. "Well she's not spending the night over there. Hell no!" I said.

Airene walked into the living room where I was sitting to confront me. "Why not?" Airene asked. "Because you don't let your children just be spending the night at everyone's house like that. Robin is only twelve years old. I trust my daughter but I don't know anything about Tajah's stepfather and her two brothers. For all we know, Tajah's father could be a sex offender or pedophile or something. Please call Robin and tell her we'll be coming to get her in twenty minutes. Please don't ever let our daughter spend the night at no one's house like that anymore, without talking it over with me first," I said.

Airene rolled her eyes at me, like I actually cared. "I know she's going to be mad to hear that she's coming home and can't spend the night," Airene said. "I don't care about her being mad or upset. It's our duty as parents to make sure that our daughter is safe at all times. We may not be able to watch her 24/7, because she's at school and we're at work but that's a different story, when we're home and she's supposed to be home too," I said.

"I don't see what the big deal is. When Akeem was a child, he spent the night at his first cousin's and friend's houses all the time." Airene said. I wanted to tell Airene that's probably exactly why Akeem acts the way he acts now but I know that would cause a huge argument, so I left it alone. "Please call her now," I said.

Airene got up and grabbed the cordless phone in the kitchen. "Hey there Joanne. How are you? Oh okay that's good. Will you tell Robin that her aunt is coming over to have dinner with us and they want to see her, so she'll have to come home tonight. Please tell her I'll be there to get her in about fifteen minutes," Airene said, hanging up the phone.

"Are you ready?" Airene asked, with an attitude. "Yes," I said, grabbing my keys off of the table. Airene didn't say anything on the ride to get Robin and neither did I. We pulled up in the yard and blew the horn. Joanne came to the door and waved at us as she let Robin out the door. We both waved back, as Robin got in the car.

"Hey Daddy, hey Mom," Robin said, as if she didn't see Airene all day. "Hey sweetheart. Look how did you get to Tajah's house?" I asked. "Oh Mrs. Joanne picked us up from school today," Robin said. I looked at Airene, like I could ring her damn neck. "So sweetheart if something was to happen to you, your mom wouldn't know what to tell the police what you were wearing, since you leave to go to school after she goes to work, right?" I asked. "I guess not," Robin said. I sat there looking at Airene, wondering how the hell is she so damn careless with her one and only daughter, just to be letting her leave school with people like that and not telling me anything of what's going on.

"So Aunt Pam is coming over for dinner tonight?" Robin asked. "No sweetheart she's not. Your Mom just said that because I guess she thought it wouldn't sound so bad, other than to say we were just coming to get you," I said. "Okay so why did you all just come and get me?" Robin asked. "Because you don't need to be spending the night at anyone's house. Anything can happen, especially with her stepfather and her two brothers living there too," I said.

I was waiting for Robin to catch her little attitude and have her little tantrum so I could give her exactly what she deserved when we got home but she didn't. "Dad, it's a good thing you did came and got me when you did," Robin said. "And why is that?" I asked. "Because her brother Reggie had three of his friends spending the night there as well and one was looking at me a little strange and he made me feel uncomfortable," Robin said. "See there! Right there is exactly what the hell I was talking about earlier. You never know who will be at a person's house for you to be letting your child be spending the night at their house like that. I don't care if it's your sister, your cousin, or your best friend. Robin, please I don't care whose house you're at, I don't ever want you spending the night at no one's house.

We don't let anyone spend the night at our house, so I don't want you spending the night at no one's house either. You never know what or who can be over there. See you had no idea that Reggie's friends were going to be over there did you?" I asked. "No sir, I didn't." Robin said. "Okay sweetheart so please don't ask us that again, okay?" I said.

"Okay Dad I won't and you're right. You can't be letting your children be spending the night at people's house like that," Robin said.

I glanced over at Airene to see what she had to say now but she had a dumbfounded look on her face, like that situation could've really been something tragic if something had happened to our daughter, from something she said was okay.

16

CHAPTER 5

"Ryan"

Pickle and I laid in bed after doing our thing. Pickle was just smiling, like he knew he just put it down, which he definitely did. I swear each time Pickle and I are together, I'm definitely always satisfied. Pickle just looked at me, with a crazy look on his face. "Why are you looking at me like that?" I asked. "Look in my wallet, where I keep my money," Pickle said.

I got up out of bed and got Pickle's wallet out of his back pants pocket and looked in it. There was a wad of nothing but one-hundred dollar bills. "Dang, this is a lot of money," I said. "It's all yours Ryan. I want you to stop doing what you're doing. Do you hear me?" Pickle said. "What am I doing?" I asked. "Come on Ryan, don't try to play me. I'm no fool," Pickle said.

I couldn't say anything, wondering how Pickle knew my side hustle job. "How did you find out?" I asked. "Come on Ryan, these little Gastonia people be talking. You think people around here don't know what you're doing and that they're talking?" Pickle asked. I thought I covered all my tracks good but obviously I haven't. "I hope that's enough for you to eventually stop doing what you're doing?" Pickle asked. "Well it's not. I need a lot more," I said.

Pickle sat up in bed and patted a spot on the bed for me to have a seat next to him. I sat down like he asked. "Look, what you're doing is dangerous. You're going to mess around and get yourself killed, or catch Aids," Pickle said. There was a look of concern in his eyes as if he really cared about me. "Ah, you act like you care about me," I said, smiling. "I do Ryan. For five years now, we've been dealing with each other and I've grown to love you man. I genuinely care about you and don't want to see anything happen to you," Pickle said.

I was actually shocked that Pickle felt that way about me and actually said it. Pickle isn't the type of guy that expresses his feelings like that, so to hear him speak that way about me made my heart beat a little faster than normal.

For once in my life, I was actually speechless. This fool actually caught me off guard and before I knew it, I actually had tears in my eyes but hold the hell up, I was so caught up in my feelings that I almost forgot that this fool actually is with my first cousin and not just with her, they're married and have three damn children together. And his ass sells damn drugs as well. What does he think he is doing, selling powdered sugar?

I know Pickle saw the expression on my face and he had to know what I was thinking. "What are your thoughts about what I just said?" Pickle asked. Well I guess he didn't read the expression I had on my face to know what I'm thinking, as if he had some kind of powers. "Pickle, I really appreciate your concern about me but you're married to my first cousin Shontel. How in the world this is going to work?" I asked.

Pickle looked at me and started laughing, like I said something funny. "Ryan look, I didn't say I wanted to date you or be in a relationship with you. I just told you that I truly love you and I care about your wellbeing, not that I'm ready to jump in a relationship or marry you or anything. "I just don't want to see anything happen to you." Pickle replied.

I guess my happily ever after moment was just shattered instantly but I definitely wasn't feeling the stepfather kind of thing either. Plus, I can only imagine the conversations my family would be having about me, that I broke up Shontel's happy home. I can definitely say that their home has never been a happy one, if he's married to her but sleeping with me.

I felt everything that Pickle said, but five thousand dollars wouldn't give me the kind of lifestyle that I want and deserve for myself. My teaching job definitely pays all my bills but it wouldn't allow me to go shopping and travel the world like I want to. "Pickle, thank you for that but I'm always protected when I do anything, I'm not killing myself behind one of these fools. I don't care how fine they are," I said.

Pickle smiled and a look of relief displayed on his face, as if now he could finally exhale. "Well I'm glad to hear that. So you're not planning on stopping anytime soon are you?" Pickle asked. "Not unless you're going to pay for the money I'm losing," I said. "How much do you make slutting out your ass like that?" Pickle asked, as if I was a piece of trash he found on the ground, that he used to wipe off dog shit from the bottom of his shoes or something.

I couldn't help but burst out laughing at Pickle's comment because if one of my regulars or a newbie said it then I wouldn't have been bothered by it so I shouldn't get upset with him, even though it made me look at him a little different. "Pickle, I make what you gave me almost a night," I said, knowing damn well I was lying. There was no damn way I could make five-thousand dollars in a night, unless escorting was my only damn job and source of income. Pickle's eyes widened when I said that, as if he was shocked. "Well I know I couldn't afford to give you that kind of money a day like that. That is a lot of money but is it worth your life?" Some of these fools are crazy as hell and It won't take anything for them to kill you," Pickle said. "Thank you Pickle for your concern but I'll be okay," I said. "Okay," Pickle said, getting up and putting his clothes back on.

After Pickle got dressed, I handed him back the money. Pickle shook his head no. "Keep it. Just look at it as me paying you for your services. You did a good job," Pickle said, walking out my bedroom door. I grabbed my robe to walk Pickle out but by the time I got to my front door, he was halfway down the stairs.

The way he was acting like I really hurt his feelings or something. He normally gives me a hug and a kiss on the cheek but he didn't even look my way as he was heading for the front door. As much as I wanted to sit here thinking about why Pickle started getting all in his feelings, I don't have time to since my next John Doe is on his way here so I need to go ahead and clean myself up.

I went and jumped in the shower and brushed my teeth again before my client gets here. The last thing I want to have bodily fluids all over me when someone else is coming over. I know this isn't the kind of lifestyle I want for myself but the money is just too good for me to leave and walk away from it all. As long as it's coming in and I'm handsome enough to keep getting it, then that's exactly what I'm going to do.

I sprayed a little cologne on and rubbed it into my chest and around my pubic area, when I heard a knock on my door. "I guess it's show time" I said, heading to open the door to let my client come on in.

CHAPTER 6
"Robert"

Airene just finished washing dishes after dinner. She made a chicken and broccoli casserole, which was pretty good. Airene has never been a great cook or anything but I'll give her an "A" for today for getting it right.

When we first got married, she admitted to me that her ex-husband did all the cooking, so she never really learned how to cook. Airene's aunt Mrs. Ella raised her after her mother died when she was eight years old. Airene said she had an okay childhood growing up but it was horrible, until her aunt took her and her three other siblings in when her father killed her mother.

Airene doesn't really talk about her childhood and family much, just her siblings. Her aunt Ella raised them all. Airene said that her father was a very dangerous and abusive man, that constantly abused their mother every chance he got. Airene said her father was so bad that he would hit their mother in front of company and in front of them when he was drunk.

Airene told me her father had no compassion or love for their mother at all. She said she prayed that if she was to ever get married, that God wouldn't give her a man like her father but that's exactly what she got in her first marriage.

Airene said when she divorced her first husband, she moved far away, just so she wouldn't run up into him or see any of his family members in the stores or anything. Airene said she's seen some of her ex-husband's ways in Akeem and that scares her to death. She told me after she left her husband, one day Akeem and this guy got into it. Airene said the guy pushed Akeem and Akeem knocked the guy on the ground and started stomping him like he was killing something on the ground.

I told Airene that Akeem has to get some help because if he doesn't, that demon is probably going to be in him for the rest of his life. I'm surprised that Akeem is even staying with his father but I guess he had nowhere else to go since I kicked him out of our house for not trying to get a damn job and clean up behind himself.

I got up to check on Robin to see if she was already in the bed, which she was as she looked so peaceful. I wanted to call Ryan and see what he was up to but since it was kind of late and I knew he had to go to work in the morning, I decided to just wait until tomorrow to talk to him.

I sat in the chair next to Robin's bed gazing at her while she slept. It's amazing how I have two children and they're nothing like me. Ryan is the spitting image of me but is totally different though. Ryan is a thirty year old seventh grade science teacher and has so many qualities going for himself but yet he has so many strikes against him as well.

Ryan is smart, funny, handsome, has a wonderful personality. Ryan is gay and I think he's really out there. I always knew that he was gay ever since he was a child. I would buy Ryan GI Joe men, Legos, blocks as a child but for some reason he never wanted to play with them. Most of the things I bought him would still be in the box as if it was brand new and he never took it out of the container.

I remember my sister Veronica and her two children would come from New York to visit us and when they left my sister called me the next day and said that my niece Diamond couldn't find her baby doll and that she didn't know if she left it at my house.

I looked around in the house in the guest room that she slept in with my sister but couldn't find it. I looked under the bed, all in the closet and under the dresser, as well as all the dresser drawers in the room and still couldn't find it.

I then went to check Ryan's room and I found the doll in the bottom of his closet underneath some clothes. I didn't say anything about it but later when Ryan came home from school, I asked him if he saw it, and he told me no that he hadn't seen it.

I wanted to tell Ryan that I knew he had it but I couldn't. The fear Ryan had in his eyes thinking that I knew he had it and what I might do to him, broke my heart. I never wanted to make my son afraid of me and if that was something he was dealing with, I wanted him to feel comfortable and not afraid to come talk to me about it.

That look Ryan had in his eyes made me take a total different approach with him. Instead of hating him or trying to beat it out of him, like some fathers would probably do, I tried to invest more time in getting him involved with more sports and doing things with him. I felt that would help him want to do it and not just because I tried to force him to doing it.

Ryan did like football, even though he never wanted to play in school but he loved basketball and baseball. Ryan would be outside playing basketball all night long if his mother and I would let him. Ryan never really liked crowds or people around him. He was content being by himself in his room with a book in his hand, or playing basketball alone.

On the weekends, I would take Ryan to the YMCA and he joined the community basketball team there. The coach told me that it was amazing how Ryan could dribble and play like he was born with a basketball in his hand. I couldn't stop smiling because I finally found a sport that my son enjoyed playing that was actually a masculine sport.

Ryan played basketball all through middle school and through high school. Ryan was so good that his basketball coach in high school said that Ryan could actually get a full basketball scholarship to basically any college he wanted to go to.

All of a sudden Ryan just didn't want to play basketball anymore. I never knew why because he was so good at it. I had all kinds of trophies when Ryan made the State Championship for his school and all. I asked Ryan why he stopped playing basketball and he told me he only played because of the way I lit up when he had the ball in his hand. He said that was the only time I ever acted like I was proud of him and if he was going to get that kind of reaction out of me, then he was going to continue playing basketball, no matter how much he didn't like it or how much he hated it, he was just glad for the proud look I showed on my face when he had a basketball in his hand.

I told Ryan to never do something like that again. I would never want him to give up his own happiness or finding something that he's good at to do something that he thinks will make me happy. I told Ryan even if I don't like his hobbies, doesn't mean I can't be happy for him for doing what he enjoys.

I've learned to love all of Ryan, the good, the bad and the ugly. I used to find myself just staring at him sometimes, wondering why someone as handsome and as talented as Ryan is could end up being "gay." That was a word I could never make myself say about my son but I knew it was the truth and I had to accept it because the last thing I was going to do was make my son feel like I didn't love him and he ended up trying to kill or hurt himself because he didn't feel loved by his parents, or like we didn't want him around.

Ryan's mother and I just learned how to just love and accept him for who he is and not for who or what we were trying to make him into. Ryan and Alexandria were extremely close, that sometimes I would get a little jealous of just how close those two were.

I remember when Ryan and I were watching a football game on TV and someone knocked on the front door. I got up and opened the door and the prettiest little brown-skinned girl was standing at my door, asking to see Ryan. I went and got Ryan from off the couch to see what the young girl wanted with him, she wanted to ask Ryan to their Junior Prom.

Ryan acted like her asking him was no big deal to him so he just casually said yes. I was so proud of Ryan that I was smiling the entire day. I took Ryan to get his haircut that Thursday and took him to get a tuxedo. I got my car washed and waxed for him for his first prom.

I gave Ryan one-hundred dollars and told him I wasn't going to give him a curfew that night. I reached in the little special bag that I got for Ryan and gave him a box of condoms just in case. The look Ryan gave me, almost made me choke. Ryan had that expression on his face like, "Dad, what in the world was I going to do with those?"

After Ryan left for the prom I told Alexandria what I did while she was lying down in bed and she had to sit up because she was laughing so hard. I told Alexandria that you can't blame a father for trying.

I got up and kissed Robin on the forehead and closed her bedroom door. Airene was laying in the bed as I climbed in beside her. "What were you doing all that time, Rob?" Airene asked. "Nothing, just watching my baby girl sleeping, while thinking about her and Ryan," I said. "Why Ryan?" Airene asked. "Because that's my son," I said. "Yes I know but Ryan is a grown man, you shouldn't be thinking about him that much," Airene said.

I sat up in bed and just looked at Airene before I turned the lamp off. I couldn't believe that she actually said that to me about my own son. It was on the tip of my damn tongue to curse Airene's ass all the way out for that comment but instead, I took the high road and didn't respond and curse her out like I was about to do, but I decided to address her comment as a mature adult.

"Airene, a real parent never stops loving and thinking about their children. It doesn't matter how old they are," I said, turning over to cut the lamp off.

Airene knew she pissed me off with her last comment she just made. She tried to cuddle up against my body but I refused to let her. "It's a little too hot for that tonight," I said, turning my back towards her.

CHAPTER 7
"Ryan"

I looked at the clock and turned the music off. It's too late for me to still be up at twelve-o'clock, knowing I have to get up in the morning for work. My last client was at eleven-thirty, so I had to shower again, hopefully for the last time. I turned over in bed and said my prayers. Most people told me for the lifestyle I'm living, they're shocked that I still prayed to God.

I hate the judgment that people put on me but my mother always said, "if it walks like a duck and looks like a duck, then it's a duck." That's definitely one thing that I love and miss about my mom, she was definitely real and had no problem speaking her mind. If I had a shirt on that my mom hated, she was definitely going to tell me to take my shirt off and put another one on.

I felt the tears as they rolled down my face, just missing my mom. My mother was definitely a wonderful person and I wish I could talk to her just to hear her voice telling me to get my butt up if I overslept or something. I wish my stepmother was more loving and a little more kind to me. Mrs. Airene just seems a little too messy to me, like she likes to stir up some drama and I'm not for that. I'll be ready to slice her throat if she gets up in my face.

It seems like I wasn't really tired but my body was. I just laid in bed, hoping that sleep would eventually find me. I was still a little shocked at Pickle today when he told me he loved me. Pickle is a great, caring person with a kind heart but I could never fall in love with someone like him. I do believe that Pickle would do anything for me if he could but he couldn't afford to take care of my lifestyle with a wife and three children.

I thought about my Dad and that we missed a day without talking and texting. My Dad and I are really close and I'm happy to have such a supporting father in my life that loves me and is always there for me. I'll probably go by there to have dinner or something with him today when I get off.

I was finally able to fall asleep, when I heard someone knocking on the front door. "Who the hell is that knocking on my door at one in the damn morning," I said to myself, barely able to walk to the door. I went to the door. "Who is it?" I yelled. "No one said anything. "Who is it?" I asked again. Still no one said anything. I opened the door and looked around and the person jumped between my door, knocking me down to the floor. "Get your punk ass up!" the man yelled.

I stood up off the floor, as the man grabbed me by my pajama shirt. "How many of these guys ran up in you tonight?" the man yelled. Before I could say anything the man slapped me across my face, as if he felt like I stole something from him. The sting was extremely painful. "Get in your room and shut the fuck up!" the man said angrily.

I walked in my room and closed the door behind us. "Take off your clothes and hurry the hell up!" the man yelled. I took off my clothes like the man said. "Now lay across the bed and you better not make a damn sound!" the man said, as I felt something pointed at the side of my head, like a gun. I didn't try to put up a fight or anything, not knowing what this guy was capable of doing to me. If I just lay here and not do anything then maybe, he'll hurry up and leave and get the hell out of my house.

I tried to imagine happy thoughts of my parents when I was a child and didn't have to worry about anything. I thought about my mom and how she used to tuck me in at night and read me my favorite bedtime story, "The Little Engine That Could," and how I would laugh when Mom made the Choo-Choo sound with her mouth as she acted like she was pulling on the horn with her hand.

I thought about the day I brought my report card home in the eighth grade for the first nine weeks with all "A's." My mom and dad were so happy and excited and it made me feel good to know they were proud of me for all my hard work.

I thought about Thursday before my junior prom, when my

Dad took me to the mall to pick up my tuxedo and took me to get my hair cut and how proud he was when he was helping me tie my bowtie and helping me with my cufflinks.

It was moments like that, that was helping me bear the pain of what was happening to me as my body was being invaded by someone that wasn't invited into my home but barged their way in and took something that was mine and mine alone. How does this person think this was okay to treat me like this, as if I was nothing and when he's done, just toss me aside like I was simply an old pair of jeans or sweater that he would soon kick on the floor when he knew he wasn't going to wear it anymore?

My tears continued as he continued to thrust his body against mine, allowing the pain to pierce my body. How is this different for me for being an escort and having sex with men for money, compared to what was happening to me now? I had a choice to say "yes" or to say "no" but right now I don't.

They didn't ask me if I was okay or if they were too rough or anything. He didn't give two fucks about me. All this bastard wanted was his little happy little ending that's coming, as if it's their reward or something for putting in the time and work.

My body started to tense up and I felt like my body was about to just break down on me, which would probably be a good thing. "Oh damn! Oh damn!" the man yelled, as he was able to release himself and then turned over off of me. I felt a little relief when I saw the condom wrapper on the right side on the floor, so at least I knew he did use a condom but did I really know? Just because I saw the wrapper on the floor, doesn't mean he actually used one. "Lord, please let this bastard have a condom on! Please!" I said to over and over in my head.

This disgusting, worthless human being finally got up off of me and removed the condom from himself and laid it on top of my bed. He then walked to my bathroom and grabbed a washcloth from the linen closet to clean himself off. He started doing something as if he was looking in his wallet for something. He then threw something on top of my dresser and then walked out. The man didn't utter a damn word to me before leaving.

I guess there was nothing really to say to each other, since he got what he wanted. I ran over to lock my front door and then grabbed my robe and towel and took a shower to cleanse my body of the impurities that bastard just did to my body. As I was washing my body, trying to clean myself from what just happened to me, I just sat in the tub as the water from the shower just ran over my face.

This isn't something that I wanted for myself. I never dreamed I would be a science teacher with a thriving career but also have a secret life, that many people didn't know about. I'm really killing myself. I have to get out of this, one way or another and I'd rather do it while I'm still alive.

I dried myself off and put on my pajamas and walked back in my bedroom. I glanced on top of my dresser and looked at the money that was just thrown on the top of my dresser. The man left me three thousand dollars.

I folded up the money and put it with the rest of my little stash that I've been saving, since I started doing this escorting thing five months ago. I'm almost at my goal of getting what I want so I can be done with this lifestyle all together because the next time, I may not be as lucky to walk away like I did tonight.

CHAPTER 8
"Robert"

I sat at my desk, looking over the few file claims. I had to call a few insurance companies to report my investigations of some of the claims that were fraud. Some of the agent's managers were so furious to learn what their clients had done, just to get a big check and some of these clients, they've had for years. After the insurance companies cut them as a client, I'm sure they'll probably file charges as well.

I wonder why so many people think they can get away with filing a false claim with the insurance companies. I guess everyone is out just trying to get a quick buck and they don't care how illegal it is. I'm sure they'll see when the police comes knocking at their door or picks them up from their jobs. How embarrassing will that be to be escorted off the job premises by police officers and taken to jail.

I just hung up the phone with Farm Bureau, when someone knocked on my office door. "Come in," I said, not looking up to see who it was. "Good morning Mr. Robert. Here's your morning coffee and your glazed doughnut," Shannon said, placing it on top of my desk. "Thank you Shannon," I replied. "No problem. What are you doing this weekend?" Shannon asked, just as I took a big bite out of my doughnut.

I chewed up the piece of doughnut I bit into before I responded back to Shannon. "Well, I'll probably take Robin to the movies or something. I heard her talking to one of her friends, saying she couldn't wait to see "Bad Boys III," so I think I'll surprise her and take her and her best friend out there and to grab something to eat afterwards," I said.

Shannon smiled and placed her hand over her heart as if my

statement touched her or something. "Mr. Robert, you are such a wonderful father. I sure hope your daughter and son, knows how wonderful you are as a father," Shannon said. "Well, if they don't, I try to remind them, every chance I get," I said, laughing. "I know that's right. Lord, I sure hope one day I meet a handsome man like you that loves me as well as his children, if he has some," Shannon said. "I'm sure you will meet Mr. Right very soon," I said.

Shannon burst out laughing when I made that comment. "Why are you laughing?" I asked, wondering why Shannon burst out laughing like that wasn't possible or something. "Because, I'll settle for Mr. Just Right Now, instead of Mr. Right," Shannon said, laughing. I burst out laughing as well, almost spitting out my coffee all over the place. "Who knows, maybe you can introduce me to your son one day. If he's anything as handsome as his father, then I definitely want to meet him," Shannon said.

This time, I almost choked on the rest of my doughnut when Shannon made that statement. "Are you okay?" Shannon asked. "Yes I am. You just almost made me choke when you mentioned my son. Trust me, you would definitely be barking up the wrong tree then," I said, wiping my mouth with my napkin. "Why is that? Is he married or in a relationship or something?" Shannon asked. "No, nothing like that. Ryan just wouldn't be interested," I said, not trying to put my son's business out there or anything.

The look Shannon just gave me, I knew she was about to start rolling her neck and eyes, at my comment. "So you think I'm not good enough for your son or that your son wouldn't like me or something? Am I that ugly Mr. Robert?" Shannon asked.

I knew there was simply no other way to put this conversation to rest until I tell Shannon the truth one way or the other. "Shannon sweetheart, my son is gay. He's not interested in any women, so trust me when I say it wouldn't be just you, it wouldn't be anyone that has lady parts," I said, hoping that Shannon finally got the real picture now.

Shannon quickly covered her mouth, like she just put her foot down there, which she certainly did. "Oh my God Mr. Robert. I'm so sorry about that. I didn't know. Let me get my behind back to my desk and do some work," Shannon said. "Certainly," I replied, glad that Shannon had finally let this conversation go.

I just shook my head at Shannon but I couldn't help but laugh at myself. Shannon is definitely a beautiful woman and I would love to see Ryan settle down with someone like her but I know that will never happen. I do wish that Ryan would meet someone nice and be in a stable relationship with them. I know it wouldn't be a woman but at least I'll know he's with someone that at least makes him happy.

Ryan is the spitting image of me so I would definitely say he's quite handsome. People have often told me that Ryan looks like Taye Diggs but just a little bigger. Ryan works out a lot so he is a lot more muscular and toned than I am. All the young ladies were always running behind Ryan at church, always wanting to go out with him. He's even had a few older women, that knew their old behinds should've sat down somewhere, running behind my son, who's half their age.

I pray for my family every night but I especially pray for Ryan all the time. Something tells me that Ryan is doing a lot of things that he knows I wouldn't approve of. I guess that's why I took out a large insurance policy out on him in case something was to happen to him, I'll have enough money to bury him and I won't have to break my bank account doing so.

I'm sure Ryan has all of that in order though. He's always been the type to be ahead of things like that. After Alexandria's death, I made sure Ryan was well taken care of and his education would be paid for in full. Ryan was able to get an academic scholarship to attend UNC Charlotte NC, so that helped out tremendously.

I finished up all my reports and finished contacting all the insurance companies to give them my feedback after I finished my investigation. I've been a fire investigator for almost thirty years and it has its perks at times, but then again, it could be quite boring and frustrating as well, not to mention stressful. Sometimes, I have to just stop working in my office and take a little stroll in the building and outside, just to clear my head and get away from my office and computer for a little while.

I looked down at my watch and saw it was only five minutes until lunch time. I forgot my lunch at home, from rushing that I guess I'll have to pick up something from somewhere. I was just about to pull up the "Smoke Pit BBQ," menu, when I heard a knock on my office door. "Come in," I said.

Shannon opened my door and walked in. "Oh Lord, wonder what she wants now. Maybe she's about to tell me that she thinks she can convert Ryan back to being straight of something," I thought to myself as I smiled. "What's up Shannon," I tried to say as cheerful as possible. "What are you doing for lunch? I was wondering if you would let me take you out for lunch?

I know I probably made a spectacle of myself earlier and that would be my way of an apology if you would allow me to take you out for lunch?" Shannon said. I managed to crack a smile to Shannon's invitation. As much as I wanted to say no and tell her this wouldn't be a good idea, I wondered why not? A free lunch? I'm not that crazy to turn that shit down. "Well Shannon, you don't have to do that. All is forgiven, I promise but I'm not going to turn down your invitation," I replied, smiling. "Well good. What do you have a taste for?" Shannon asked. "Maybe a turkey sub from Substation," I said. "Oh good, I was thinking about getting a salad from there. Would you like to go now?" Shannon asked. "Yes that's fine. Just give me a few seconds to shut down my computer," I said. "Okay, I'll go get my purse," Shannon said.

I cut off my computer and put all my files and documents away. The last thing I needed was for someone to come in my office, picking up files on my desk, getting me in trouble. I grabbed my car keys and my blazer and put it on. "Are you ready?" I asked, closing my office door and walking toward the front desk. "Yes Mr. Roberts," Shannon said, as we walked to my car.

I don't know how this would look to people if they were to see me and Shannon riding in the same car and having lunch together. You know people can make a hill into a mountain, if you give them some time. It should be okay for two people to have lunch together, despite them being the opposite sex and one is married and the other isn't. Maybe our lunch would be us not running up into anyone from the job or someone I know.

CHAPTER 9
"Ryan"

I just got to work and I could barely keep my eyes open. I didn't actually fall asleep until about two-thirty, knowing I had to get up at six-thirty to prepare myself for work. I knew I was going to catch pure hell this morning, trying to stay away so I did the next best thing I could think of, to catch a little nap. I stuck a movie in and told the class they needed to write me a one-and-a-half-page essay, telling me what they got out of the movie by the end of class.

I propped my hand against my face and before I knew it, I was asleep. I was sleeping so hard that I didn't know that Ms. Smith, the principal just walked in my classroom, without knocking. I jumped when I heard the book slammed on the floor. I looked up as Ms. Smith was looking in the direction the book fell.

I knew God laid it on Shamani's heart to slam her book down on the floor, because I'm sure she knew I was asleep. "Hey, Ms. Smith, what can I do for you?" I asked. "Oh, I was just coming by to check on my teachers to see what their classes were doing. I see you have your class watching a movie this morning, huh?" Ms. Smith asked. "Yes ma'am I do," I replied.

Mrs. Smith picked up the DVD carton off my desk, as she examined it and then laid it back down. "So they're studying diseases Mr. Jacobs?" Ms. Smith asked. "Yes ma'am they are. I'm teaching them the importance of diseases, safety protection equipment, with working with hazardous chemicals, labels of all kinds," I said. "Oh I see," Ms. Smith said, looking straight at me, as if I was lying to her.

"What are they writing down?" Ms. Smith asked. They're doing an essay on what they got out of the movie," I said. "Oh okay. Well

I won't keep them from their movie. You have a great day," Ms. Smith said, walking out my classroom. I took a deep breath and slowly exhaled, grabbing my chest. Ms. Smith almost caught me sleeping in my own classroom. If she had, she definitely would've fired me on the spot. I'm so grateful to Shamani for what she did. I'll have to give her five dollars for helping a brother out. No I don't think I'll do that, especially if someone sees me handing her money. People might get the wrong idea.

The movie had about ten more minutes left, just in time before the bell rings. "I hope everyone is almost done with their essay?" I said. No one said anything so I take it that no one is almost done. You need to turn your essay in before you leave today," I said.

The bell just rang and everyone brought their essay up and laid it on top of my desk. Shamani came up to me and handed her essay to me. "Mr. Jacobs, I hope you get you some rest because you were fast asleep in class. You know if Ms. Smith saw you sleeping, she would've fired you. I didn't want that to happen, so that's why I slammed my book on the floor, to wake you up. Mr. Jacobs, please get you some rest," Shamani said, with a smile on her face as she walked out of my classroom.

Shamani sounded concerned, like she genuinely cared and didn't want to see me lose my job or anything. I went to the cafeteria and got a cup of coffee. Maybe that will help me to stay awake until I get off from work. The coffee helped a great deal and I managed to stay awake the rest of the day.

I got off from work and called my Dad and talked to him for a while. Dad invited me over for dinner and I told him I was definitely going to come. I went home and took a little nap just so I wouldn't be tired and sleepy at their house. My alarm clock went off, letting me know it was time for me to get prepared to have dinner at Dad and Airene's house tonight.

I jumped in the shower and got dressed. As I was getting dressed, Jarod stuck his head in my door. "Hey Ryan, are you busy?" Jarod asked. "No, I can talk. I'm just getting ready to head to my Dad's house for dinner, but I have time to talk. So what's up?" I asked. "Oh nothing man. I just wanted to tell you that I have your rent money," Jarod said, handing me his portion of the rent money, as well as the bill money as well. "Thank you Jarod, but remember I told you that this is your last month being late, I just can't do it anymore," I said.

"I understand," Jarod said, standing up and heading out the door. I'm glad Jarod finally paid his rent and hopefully I won't have to deal with that issue with him again. I grabbed my keys and headed out the door.

I pulled up in my Dad's driveway, where he used to live with my mother and I. Man, we were so happy back then. I had to put that thought in the back of my head and plan to start my day. I rang the doorbell and waited for someone to come to the door.

I saw my Dad peek out the window and then he opened the door. "Hey Ryan. It's good to see you son," Dad said, as he hugged and kissed me on the cheek. "Hey Dad. It's good to see you as well," I said. "Well come on in and have a seat. Airene is just about to finish with dinner," Dad said. "Okay," I said, following Dad in the living room.

Dad looked like he was glad to see me and couldn't stop smiling. "So son, how's work coming along? "Dad asked. "It's good, besides the bad behind kids just being bad," I said. "Oh okay," Dad said, laughing. "How's your job? You haven't had anyone trying to come beat you up yet have you?" I asked, laughing. "Oh no man and besides that, your Dad is always packing heat at all times," Dad said, taping his side. I burst out laughing because Dad is always ready to shoot somebody, knowing damn well he doesn't have a gun.

Airene came in the living room where we were sitting. "Hey Ryan, I didn't know you were out here. Your father told me you were coming over for dinner but I didn't know you were already here," Airene said, as she extended her arms out to hug me. I stood up and gave her a hug. Airene was just doing that in front of my Dad, she knows she doesn't like me like that but I was going to behave myself tonight and not let this woman get me upset tonight.

"Everything is done so you guys can all wash your hands and you can go ahead and fix your food or I could fix it if you want,"

Airene said. "Well, if it's not a problem, you can go ahead and fix mine. I don't want to be greedy and fix too much," I said. "Well I don't mind but you can have as much as you want Ryan. That's not a problem at all," Airene said.

I don't know if Airene is actually serious or just full of it because Dad is around. I've seen her in the grocery store and Walmart and Airene would walk right past me, as if she didn't see me, so I'm aware of how fake and phony she can be.

I washed my hands and went into the kitchen. "Dad, where is Robin?" I asked. "She's coming now," I just told her you were here and you were going to have dinner with us. Robin must have had a rough day because she was knocked out in her bed, like she has a normal 9 to 5 job or something," Dad said, laughing. I laughed because I definitely knew how that is, since I came straight home from work and got straight in the bed and I knew I worked and was definitely exhausted.

Robin walked in the dining room, and her eyes actually lit up when she saw me. "Hey big brother. How are you doing?" Robin asked, as she gave me a big hug and I kissed her on the forehead. "I'm good. How are you doing?" I asked, as I released her from my embrace. "I'm okay but for some reason I was extremely tired today. I didn't go to bed too late last night so I don't know why I was so tired," Robin said.

Dad said the blessing and we all dove straight in. Airene is a good cook but she didn't have anything on my mom's cooking. My mom could cook so good, all you wanted to do after you were done eating was to lick your plate. Dinner looked good though. Airene made homemade beef stew, with carrots, potatoes, and a lot of mixed vegetables, over white rice. Airene even had it seasoned good as well. It wasn't salty or too spicy or anything. The food was dead on it.

We all talked a little while finishing dinner but I guess eating was what we were mostly focused on. After dinner, I hugged Robin and told her good-night and that I loved her. She smiled and told me she loved me too. "Son, you got time to have a beer with your old man, before you leave?" Dad asked. "Always," I said.

Dad went to the fridge and took out two Coors Light beers and handed one to me. We sat on the porch and Dad pulled out a jazz black & mild. I always loved the aroma from a jazz black & mild. Dad used to smoke them back in the day and Mama made Daddy brush his teeth before she would kiss him.

It seems like I always have a memory when it comes down to Mom and Dad. Some make me smile and laugh and others just make me go back and just think about life in general, of how much I just missed her. Dad and I were just enjoyed the nice mid-September night breeze, while talking and laughing about our memories of Mom that we both enjoyed.

I got up and went back in the house to go to the restroom. My Dad's and Airene's bedroom was right beside the bathroom. After I used the bathroom and was about to wash my hands, I heard Airene talking on the phone to someone. "Pam, you won't believe who came over and ate dinner with us tonight? Robert's little faggot son Ryan. Girl, that boy has gay written all over him, so Robert can sit there and pretend he doesn't know about Ryan if he wants to, but everyone does. He's not blind and neither are we," Airene said.

I stood by the door with the doorknob in my hand about to walk out when I heard Airene said my name. My feelings were crushed to hear her say those terrible things about me.

I shook my head and washed my hands and gently opened the bathroom door to go back outside but I wasn't in the mood anymore, so I knew it was time for me to go ahead and head on home. I knew I had to let Airene know that I heard her and I knew she was just as two-faced as they come.

I knocked on her already half opened bedroom door. "Hey Airene, I'm about to leave," I said. "Okay Ryan. You have a good night and drive home safely. We really enjoyed your company tonight," Airene said, with a plastered looking fake ass smile on her face, as if she thought I really believed her. "Thank you and I did as well, and Airene?" I called out her name. "Yes, Airene said, as she took the phone away from her ear." Please tell Pam, that your faggot stepson is about to leave now. Maybe she'll like to know that since you were just talking about me," I said.

Airene looked like she turned three shades lighter when I said that. I wanted her to know I heard her and now I know exactly how she felt about me. That's one thing about people, you can pretend all you want around them, making them think you're a wonderful, kind, sweet person all day long, but eventually your mask came off and the real you is revealed.

I grabbed my beer bottle and threw it in the trash and headed out the door. Dad looked up at me and smiled but I didn't smile back, I kept walking. "Dad, I think it's best for me to not come back," I said, walking toward my car.

Dad jumped up off the step and ran toward me. "Ryan, what are you talking about not coming back anymore? Did something happen?" Dad asked. I told Dad all about his little uppity, stupid ass wife and what she said about me to Pam on the phone.

Dad shook his head and it looked like his anger completely took over him. "Don't worry about her Ryan, I'll take care of her behind when you leave," Dad said. "Well, I just wanted you to know what kind of wife your married to," I said. "Stay right here for a second. Let me get you a bottle of cold water to drink on your way home," Dad said.

Dad walked in the house and returned with a bottle of water and handed one to me. "Son, I'm so sorry this happened but trust me, I'll handle it. I promise!" Dad said "Okay," I replied.

Dad grabbed me in a big bear hug and hugged me and then he kissed me on the cheek. "Ryan, I will always love you. Don't you ever forget that as long as you live," Dad said. "I won't Dad and I love you too," I replied, getting in my car.

I drove off, realizing that this was probably my last time coming here again. I can't stand fake ass, phony people, that talk in your face but the minute you turn your back, they're the first ones to talk about you. At least Airene don't have to try and pretend that she likes me, since I already know the truth about how she really feels and now my Dad knows as well.

CHAPTER 10
"Robert"

Ryan just left and my temper was through the damn roof with Airene. I walked in the house and slammed the front door. Airene was in our bedroom, still on the phone. I guess she felt that even though she said what she said and Ryan heard her, she wasn't about to end her phone conversation for anyone.

I walked up and sat on the bed, looking up in her face while she was on the phone. I just wanted to see how long she was going to sit there talking when she knew I had a bone to pick with her. Airene went in the bathroom and took a shower and brushed her teeth, while still on the phone. She finally hung up the phone when she walked back in our bedroom, to put on her pajamas.

"Hey sweetie, did you enjoy dinner tonight? I hope Ryan enjoyed it," Airene said, so casual like nothing happened. Who the hell is this woman I'm married to? How in the world you're acting like nothing happened, knowing you said what you said to my son and you're acting like it's no big deal? "Dinner was good and I'm sure Ryan enjoyed dinner as well, but he came back outside, pissed off because he heard you talking about him," I said. "Well I was talking to Pam on the phone and I guess he overheard his name but if he was doing what he's supposed to be doing in there, then he wouldn't have heard me talking about him," Ariene said, with a smirk on her face, like she didn't say anything wrong.

I just shook my head at Airene's response and just stared at her. This is really the person I married thirteen years ago? "So you think it's okay to call my son names like that, while he's still here at our house? Airene, anyone could have heard you and you're acting like you didn't do anything wrong?" I said, getting up off the bed to face her.

"Well, I can't believe I married someone as cold and heartless as you. I love my son Airene. I don't care if he's gay or not, I will never disown him or mistreat him and I won't allow you to do it either. Either you're going to treat my son with some respect or we're done,' I said. "What! So you're willing to walk away from me because I don't like what your gay ass son is doing?" Airene yelled. "No, I'm willing to walk away from you if you can't respect him and treat him like a human being," I said.

Airene just looked at me as if I was the one with the problem and I was starting an argument with her. "I can't believe you're acting like that Robert. Your son is gay and you're sitting here condoning it, like it's okay. Damn man, man the hell up!" Airene yelled. "Look Airene, I'm not condoning my son's lifestyle but he is grown and in his own house. He has a good job and he doesn't ask me for anything," I said.

"Well, I guess that's a good thing until he dies from Aids, huh?" Ariene said. Before I knew it, I grabbed her by the shoulders and I wanted to knock her ass out. I've never in my life wanted to hit a woman before but I wanted to lay her ass out on the floor. "Get your damn hands off me!" Airene screamed, as she snatched away.

I had to take a few steps back from her because I was afraid of what I might do. "What the hell is wrong with you, putting your hands on me!" Airene yelled. "I'm sorry, I shouldn't have done that," I replied. "No you shouldn't have," Airene yelled, rolling her eyes.

I knew the longer I stayed here going back and forth with Airene, the more things were going to really spiral out of control, so I knew the best thing for me to do was just leave. I grabbed my suit and a few things I would need in the morning and brought it in the guest room because I knew I couldn't sleep in the same room with this woman after she showed me who she is.

I sat on the bed for a few minutes, knowing I had some things still brewing inside of me that I needed to get off my chest. I went back to the room to confront Airene. Airene was lying in the bed as if we didn't just have a heated argument that she caused.

I stood there just looking at her. I knew what I had to say was only going to add more fuel to the fire but I had to say it. "I don't believe you," I said. Airene opened her eyes and looked over in my direction. "What is it now Robert? You want to come blame me some more for the horrible word that I called your little princess earlier? You still mad about that? You want to come in here and beat me up now?" Airene said, now sitting up in the bed.

I couldn't believe how Airene was acting. She acted like Ryan disrespected her or something, which he didn't. Is she on something for the reason she's acting so heartless and cold? "What do you want now?" Airene asked. "I just wanted to tell you that I'm not perfect and neither is Ryan but he's a good person. Now I'm sitting here thinking about my son, compared to yours and you have no right to say anything negative about Ryan. Your son doesn't even work. He stayed here for six months and had five jobs that he might have stayed at for three weeks total the entire time. Your trifling ass son would eat up all the food in the house and smoke weed all in here, even when we asked him not to and he wouldn't even clean up behind himself. Now my son is a teacher and a successful teacher at that, with a Master's degree. My son has his own house and his own car. Ryan doesn't have to ask to borrow our car to supposedly go look for a job, which they never found and then use up all the damn gas in the car, lying saying they were going job hunting. All that was your son. Your son was the one that's been in and out of jail basically his entire life.

So you have the damn nerve to talk about my son, like your son is perfect or something and he's nothing but a damn loser, just like your damn ex-husband. So before you start judging my son about his sexuality, maybe you should look at your own son before you start judging mine." I said.

I walked back in the guestroom and got in the bed. I said everything I had to say. I knew I needed to pray before I close my eyes tonight but the way I'm feeling right now; I definitely didn't feel like doing it but I forced myself to get up.

I closed my eyes to pray, "Dear God, I thank you for everything. I thank you for my life, my children, and even my insane wife. I don't know what's going on with her but I do love her. God, please continue to watch over my family, my job and my household. Lord please, please watch over Ryan. Lord, I know Ryan is out there and really, really out there but I'm asking you to please watch over him and keep him in your protection. Amen" I said, as I got in the bed.

CHAPTER 11
"Ryan"

I just got home and jumped in the shower. I was still fuming and ready to shoot up something. I can't believe my stepmother said that about me but to be honest, I knew she never really cared for me anyway. I would at least have thought she would've waited until I left their house before she started talking about me to someone on the phone. Maybe I'm not living my life right but it's not her place to judge me, like she's perfect or something. I know she doesn't have to worry about me stepping foot in her house again.

I got out of the shower and dried myself off. I put on my pajamas and got in the bed. I felt so tired that I knew it wouldn't be hard for me to fall asleep. I knew before I go to bed, I need to say my prayers because after the night I just had, I needed to call on the Lord's name.

I got on my knees and closed my eyes. "Father God, thank you for my health, life and strength. I thank you for waking me up this morning in my right mind. I thank you for your protection and for my Dad and my little sister. I'm asking you to watch over them both. Lord, I know I didn't have the best night over at my Dad's and stepmother's house. My stepmother said something horrible about me and I overheard it and went off on her. Lord forgive me for what I said and forgive her for what she said. Keep us all God in your mercy and your care. Amen."

My alarm went off and I jumped up, grabbing my things and got in the shower. I'm glad I took my clothes out last night so all I have to do is iron my shirt and put everything on. I grabbed my keys and turned off the lights. I'm a little early for work, which is a good thing.

I was heading to my class when I walked into this guy walking down the hallway, with a black suit on. "Good morning Mr. Jacobs. How are you?" Ms. Smith asked. "I'm doing well. I want you to meet Mr. Lawrence Eaddy. Mr. Eaddy just got the position as the new assistant principal here." Ms. Smith said. "Good morning Mr. Eaddy. I'm Ryan Jacobs and I teach seventh grade Science," I said. "Nice to meet you," Mr. Eaddy said. "Nice to meet you as well. Let me get to my class. You both have a great day," I said, heading down the hall to my class.

I can't believe that Lawrence is here at my damn school as the new assistant principal. Lawrence and I use to mess around about four years ago, until he got married. Lawrence isn't the most attractive man but the sex was the bomb. I walked to my class and sat at my desk. I looked at my watch, realizing I have five minutes before the kids come in.

I sprayed Lysol in the air and sprayed each desk and then wiped them off. The kids walked in and sat down at their desk. "Good morning Mr. Jacobs," the kids said. "Good morning class. Everyone please take your seats and take out your text book and Bradly please read the first two paragraphs on page one-twenty, in Chapter sixteen?" I said. "No sir. I don't feel like reading," Bradly said. "Well, I wasn't asking you to. It's more of a statement so please read the first two paragraphs for me," I said again. "I said No!" Bradly yelled, knocking his book down on the floor and getting up, walking out of my class.

I wasn't about to run behind Bradly since he walked out like that. He must know where he's going since he just left my class. "Latonia, will you please read the first two paragraphs for me and then the next person and just go down the line, reading two paragraphs each," I said. "Sure," Latonia said as she began reading.

I took out my disciplinary forms and wrote Bradly up for his insubordination and him abandoning my class. "Keya, can you please come up here?" I asked. "Yes," Keya said, as she walked towards me. "Can you please take this to the office?" I asked, not wanting to leave the class unattended. Keya nodded her head and took the disciplinary form from me.

The students continued reading while I had to get my thoughts together about what just happened. I wonder why Bradly acted like that? He's never given me any problems before. Bradly has always been quiet but very respectful. It wasn't like I asked him to read the entire chapter, only the first two paragraphs. I know I didn't embarrass him or anything. Maybe Bradly can't read and he thought I was making fun of him or something, which was definitely not the case.

After class I walked down to the office to talk with Ms. Smith. Ms. Smith and Lawrence were sitting in her office when she saw me. She waved me inside. "Hey Mr. Jacobs, I see you had quite a morning with Bradly James huh?" Ms. Smith asked. "Yes, I don't know what got into Bradly this morning. The way he stormed out of my classroom, isn't like him at all. I think there was something more to why he refused to read this morning when I asked him," I said. "Well, maybe it's something to investigate instead of me suspending him for what he did," Ms. Smith said.

I nodded my head at her comment, "I'll call to speak with his mother this afternoon and if I can't get in touch with her, I'll go by her house too," I said. "Okay well that's good," Ms. Smith said.

I stood up to walk out of Ms. Smith's office and Lawrence was staring at me from head to toe, as if he's never seen me before or something. "You both have a great day," I said, heading back to my class.

I walked to my classroom, just as the bell was about to ring. I closed the door and as I was walking towards my desk, I heard someone knocking on my classroom door. I turned around and saw that it was Bradly. I was going to let Bradly in but I figured it wouldn't be a smart thing to do since he walked out on his class to come to another one. The students were just staring, wondering why Bradly was knocking on the door like that. I took my cell phone out and called Ms. Smith. "Hello," Ms. Smith answered. "Ms. Smith, Bradly is outside my classroom knocking on the door like he's going crazy," I said. "Well, do you think you should answer the door and let him in?" Ms. Smith asked. "No! I don't know what Bradly is capable of doing or has planned. I have to ensure the children's safety as well as myself," I said. "Okay, you're right," Ms. Smith said.

I hung up the phone and Bradly finally stopped knocking like some maniac and left. I will admit that I was scared as hell because you never know what a person is capable of doing when they're upset and I wasn't about to jeopardize my students lives and safety by letting Bradly back in my class, not knowing what he was going to do. I hope whatever is going on with Bradly that he'll be okay.

CHAPTER 12
"Robert"

I got up this morning and made breakfast for Robin and I. "Daddy, are you okay?" Robin asked. "Yes, I'm okay baby. Why do you ask?" I said. "I heard you and Mom arguing about Ryan last night. Daddy, Mama was definitely wrong about what she said about Ryan, especially while he was still here. I know Ryan is gay but he is still my brother and I still love him," Robin said. "Thank you sweetheart," I replied.

I agreed with everything Robin was saying but I wasn't about to discuss what Airene and I are going through with my twelve-year-old daughter. "Thanks babe," I said. Robin and I ate our breakfast not saying much. Airene came in the kitchen and grabbed a paper towel. "Good morning," Airene said. "Good morning," Robin and I replied. Airene grabbed a plate and fixed her breakfast. I was still very much pissed off with her and I don't have anything to say to her right now. Airene tried to make conversation but I just started scrolling on Facebook, just so we wouldn't have to engage in conversation or look at each other. I glanced at the time and saw it was almost that time for me to be heading out to work. "You all have a great day," I said, kissing Robin on the forehead and heading out the door.

Airene and I can really act like children when we're upset with each other but this time she was dead ass wrong for what she said about Ryan. I grabbed my things from off the passenger side and headed into the building. Shannon was putting some things in the file cabinet." Good morning Mr. Robert. How are you doing?" Shannon asked. "Good morning Shannon, I'm fine. How are you?" I asked. "Oh I'm okay," Shannon replied, with a warm smile. I'm glad to hear that," I said, opening my office door.

I sat down at my desk and closed my eyes for a few seconds. I have to pull myself together just to make it through the day. It just felt like I had so much weighing on me and I was ready to free myself from it all. Maybe a weekend trip to the beach or something. I'll have to hit up Myron and Shelvin and see if they're free this weekend. I think a boy's trip is exactly what I need.

I had three fire inspections that I have to schedule sometime this week. It amazes me how many people are setting these fires on purpose, just to get some insurance money out of it. As long as I've been doing this, I can detect an accidental fire a mile away from an intentional fire. I took out my cell phone to text Ryan to see how his day was going. Ryan responded that he was doing good and he hope I was having a good day as well. I told Ryan that my day was going pretty good but I wanted to check on him to see if he was okay, since the other night. Ryan got a little quiet but finally responded back after twenty minutes later, telling me he was fine. I could tell he was still upset but I told him to be him and not worry about what people say. He responded back saying "Okay." I guess Ryan felt like that was okay if he had to stand up to people that didn't know him well but he shouldn't have to stand up against his own stepmother, with her judgment, as if she's perfect or something.

I took a deep breath to try to think about something else, just so I won't be ready to pop a blood vessel in my freaking head or something. I was just scheduling my days when I was going to come out to the homes and the companies to do my investigation, when someone knocked on my door.

I knew it was Shannon but I swear I'm not up to fool up with her today, especially since I have a lot to deal with at home and at work. "Come in," I said. Shannon walked in and sat in front of my desk, crossing her legs as if she was posing for Playboy magazine or something. "What's up Shannon? What can I do for you?" I asked, noticing how comfortable she looked in front of me, like she didn't have anything to do.

Shannon, just looked at me and smiled. "Mr. Robert, may I ask you a question?" Shannon asked. It was like I almost had to proceed with caution with Shannon for a second, because she knows she can ask me anything, so why did she feel like she needed my permission this time? "Shannon, you may ask me anything," I said. "Okay, this is my question, if a person is married and has a wife or a husband, but you know they're not happy in their marriage because the way they often look sometime and you're attracted to him or her, would you pursue them?

Now, I'm not talking about falling in love or asking them to walk away from their marriage, just some casual sex here and there from time to time. Both of the people aren't perfect by any means but this woman wants this man badly and she's willing to do all the things his wife won't do to or with him. Would you do it?" Shannon asked.

I gave Shannon the side eye for asking me a question like that but I just told her she could ask me anything she wanted to ask me. "Well, to be honest Shannon, I would have to say no, I mean the man or woman maybe unhappy in their marriage but if they feel like that and he or she feels there's just no hope, then they should just leave," I said.

"Okay. So Mr. Robert, you never cheated on your wife before?" Shannon asked. "No, I haven't," I said, knowing I was lying. "Oh okay. Well I guess you're one in a few that's never did that before. "Shannon said. "Mr. Robert do you find me attractive?" Shannon asked. "Oh Lord here we go again," I said to myself, knowing Shannon wouldn't let up if I didn't answer her question but I don't think I should. "Shannon, I don't feel comfortable answering that question," I said.

Shannon just looked at me, with a crazy look on her face, like he's really not going to answer me? To be honest, I find Shannon incredibly sexy and beautiful. Shannon is about 5'7, one hundred and eighty pounds, and has a golden, brown skin complexion. The girl is definitely built like a brick house, with everything stacked in the right places.

"Well Mr. Robert, I find you very attractive and sexy as hell. I could teach you all kinds of new tricks," Shannon said. Before I knew it, I burst out laughing. "Dang it was that funny?" Shannon asked, with a confused look on her face. "No Shannon, I'm sorry I didn't mean to laugh. "But how do you figure you can teach me some new tricks? Maybe I know everything I need to know," I said, looking at her.

Shannon burst out laughing. "Mr. Robert, everyone can learn some new things every now and then. You might show me something different that I might enjoy and I might can show you something different you might enjoy, as well. Age has nothing to do with what a person can teach you," Shannon said. "You're right," I said.

Shannon stood up from the chair in front of my desk and walked toward the door. Shannon locked the door and went to my window and closed the blinds. "What the hell," I said to myself, wondering what Shannon was up to. Shannon unbuttoned her red blouse and unzipped her dark blue skirt and let it drop to the floor.

I should stop her, hell I should definitely stop her, but my curiosity was getting the best of me and I wanted to see just how far Shannon's ass was going to take this. Shannon removed her black bra as well as her red panties, letting them both drop to the floor, like she did with her blouse and skirt a few minutes ago.

Shannon turned and looked at me while kicking off her red heels and walking towards me. I immediately got turned on and felt the stiffness in my pants. Shannon pushed my computer chair back and slid my computer keyboard and everything to the side as she sat on the top of my desk with her legs wide open, wearing nothing but a wicked smile.

I knew what I'm allowing Shannon to do inside my office is unprofessional but I must admit that I was fascinated by the view and turned on so much that If I had to stand up my manhood would probably burst a hole in my pants. Shannon took my computer chair and slid me directly up to her and trust me a brother wasn't about to put up a fight at all. This beautiful sister had me exactly where she wanted me and she knew it.

Shannon grabbed the back of my head and pulled my head down to where I was inches from her vagina. I was so close to Shannon that if I was to lick out my tongue I would be directly inside of her, tasting her juices. Shannon smelled like peaches &

crème lotion from Bath & Body works. I knew that scent from anywhere because it was my first wife, Alexandria's favorite that I always bought her for special occasions.

Just as I was about to get a little taste, she then got up and sat on my lap and started maneuvering her body back and forth on me. I felt my eyes go back in my head because I was only seconds away from exploding inside my pants.

Shannon got up quickly and walked back over to where she had her clothes lying on the floor. She put everything back on and I was so damn turned on that I wanted to snatch her ass back and tell her she's going to finish what she started but of course I couldn't do that. I was so damn pissed that she got me this excited and worked up for nothing, just to only tease me.

Shannon was now all the way dressed. She walked back to my window and opened the blinds back up and then unlocked my office door. "Mr. Robert, if you're ready for the next step, you just let me know. If you thought that was hot, trust me you haven't seen anything yet," Shannon said, as she walked out of my office.

I just sat there with my eyes closed, just to focus from the show I just received. I swear if Shannon can do all that in that amount of time, it's no telling what all she's capable of doing. This damn girl is a real, certified, hot ass freak. If I were to question that before about her, trust me when I say I definitely don't now. There's not a doubt in my damn mind that this sister here can definitely show me a good ass time but do I want her to do that?

I'm a married man and regardless of how stupid and judgmental Airene can be, she is still my wife and I'm still her husband. I can't just let anybody think they can strip down butt ass naked in front of me and think that I'm that willing to give in like that and let them have their way with me. They say curiosity killed the cat but I promise you if she was only naked for at least two more damn minutes, I was going to definitely try to destroy hers.

CHAPTER 13
"Ryan"

I just got home and jumped in the shower. Lawrence texted me earlier at work, asking me if he can come by when he gets off. I told Lawrence that time is money and money is time. I explained the situation to him and told him I don't have sex for free anymore. If you're not paying, then I'm not playing. Lawrence asked what my price was after I explained to him what I do as my little hustle. I told him five-hundred an hour and fifty dollars after every ten minutes over that hour. Lawrence told me I'm expensive and he don't know if he can afford that. I told him to hit me up whenever he gets the money because I'm not settling for anything less. Lawrence asked if he could pay two-hundred and fifty today and the rest next month when he gets paid. I told him hell no and that I was taking the money upfront when he gets here and I don't put shit on credit.

He told me he would see me at six-thirty, just enough time to get myself cleaned up and get ready. I just got out of the shower and I realized that Jarod wasn't here. Thank God because Jarod likes to give me that sinister look, "Like you gonna burst hell wide open," look, that sometimes drives me crazy. I tried to ignore him, like he's holier than thou and what I'm doing was beneath him or something.

Lawrence texted me and told me he was outside and that he was walking up now. Lawrence still dresses nice but his looks haven't changed at all, plus he gained a good bit of weight from the times we use to mess around. I know he has put on at least about thirty or forty pounds, which definitely isn't helping him out at all.

I heard he and his wife got a divorce when he thought she was going out of town and she came home two days earlier, only to catch Lawrence in bed with the piano player at their church. I burst out laughing when I heard that. I guess Lawrence said, "when the cat's away, the mice will play." I guess he had no idea that the cat was coming home way earlier than expected, therefore he didn't have time to get all his mice out the way.

I laughed as I opened the door for Lawrence. "Hey man," Lawrence said, as he gave me a hug. "What you laughing at?" Lawrence asked, as I was trying to wipe the laughter off my face. "Oh something my little sister said the other night when I was over there," I said. "Oh okay." Lawrence said, following me to my bedroom.

Lawrence started taking off his clothes and I stopped him in his tracks. "What's wrong?" Lawrence asked. "Where's my money?" I asked. "Oh, I don't quite have it all," Lawrence said. "Oh okay well how about when you get it all, then you come back because I don't do partial payments and I don't put anything on no damn credit, as I told you before. So no cash then I'm going to ask you to leave," I said, opening up my bedroom door, for Lawrence to exit my room and my house.

Lawrence stood there like he wasn't going to go anywhere. "Are you going to leave?" I asked. "Hell no! Not until I get what I can here for," Lawrence said, grabbing me and throwing me on top of the bed, as if I was a little rag doll or something that he could just manhandle. "Since you don't want to give it to me nicely, then I promise you I can be rough but either way I'm going to get what I came here for," Lawrence said, getting on top of me.

See this is why a brother always have to stay strapped because of motherfuckers like this, that think they run shit. Well, I guess I'll have to show Mr. Eaddy's ass instead of telling him. I reached under my pillow and grabbed my 9mm and cocked it before I put it to his head. "Now, I'm going to ask your bitch ass to get the fuck up off me and the fuck out of my house and don't you ever come back again!" I demanded while holding the gun in his damn face.

Lawrence jumped off the bed and started putting his clothes back on. The dude was moving so damn fast, that I'm sure he probably lost about ten pounds just how fast he was getting dressed. "Look

Ryan, I was only playing with you man. I got all the money right here," Lawrence said, pulling it all out of his pocket and counting it in front of me. "So we're good," Lawrence asked. "Hell no we're not. Get your ass up out my house. You had the damn money but what you thought that you were going to do is just pay me what you wanted to pay me and shit me out the rest right? Nah brother, we're not playing those kind of games here. So since you felt like I'm not worth the whole entire amount, then take your ass on," I said.

Lawrence walked toward the front door and stood there before he opened it. "Dang, I see you done man up and grew some balls since the last time we were getting up huh?" Lawrence asked. "Yep! I'm tired of motherfuckers trying to shit on me! Now get your ass out!" I said, slamming the door behind him as he left.

I guess I have to have a back-up plan now, so just as I was about to go on-line my cell phone ranged. Pickle's name popped up on the screen. "Hello," I answered. "What's up shorty?" Pickle asked. "I'm good. I'm home just chilling," I said. "Well I'm in the neighborhood and I need some. You up for it tonight?" Pickle asked. "Yeah, but you know I have to have my coins," I said. "Okay, I got you. I'll be there in ten minutes," Pickle said.

I grabbed my Lysol and started spraying around in my room as well as my bed, as if Pickle was going to smell Lawrence from being in here. My phone beeped letting me know I had a text message. I looked at it and Pickle was saying he was walking up now. I went and opened the front door. Pickle hugged me tightly and then he kissed me on the lips. He acted like he really missed me or something.

I looked at him with a confused look on my face. "Is everything okay? Why are you acting like this?" I asked. "I had a dream that I came over her and I found you dead, lying on the floor in a pool of blood." Pickle said. "Please Pickle don't start that again tonight," I said. "Ryan, what's it going to take for you to stop this? I can give you ten thousand dollars by Friday and you will have that to fall back on so you can stop doing this. This isn't going to turn out good for you. I've had bad dream after dream about you and none of them were good. Ryan, something bad is going to happen to you if you don't stop this lifestyle you're living. Please walk away from this because if you don't, I can't be around you anymore." Pickle said.

Pickle seems concerned about me, but it seemed like he was trying to control me. I wanted to tell him to go back home and try that controlling shit on Shontel, because her ass is the one that needs controlling but I didn't. "Look Pickle, we're all going to eventually die one day. So if mine is a little sooner than later, than I'm cool with that. At least I can say, I lived a good life," I said. "Don't you care about your Dad and your sister? I mean you sound like you're really close to them," Pickle said.

I'm not up for anymore bullshit from Pickle or Lawrence's ass or any other damn fools tonight. "Look, I'm going to bed now," I said. "You're going to bed?" Pickle said, raising his voice. "Yes, because I'm not about to do this shit with you tonight. So you take care of yourself?" I said. "So you're kicking me out huh?" Pickle asked, looking at me as if he couldn't believe it. "Yes, because I'm not wasting anymore of my time with you. So goodnight," I said.

Pickle reached in his pocket and pulled out a wad of money and threw it on the top of my dresser. "At least I'm paying you for the few minutes you lost talking with me," Pickle said. "Thank you," I said with a smirk on my face. Pickle leaned over and kissed me on the cheek and then he left. By the way Pickle looked and was acting, I can tell this was probably going to be my last time seeing him. Well if he feels that's best, I'm not about to cry and drool over his ass. Mama always said, "If someone wants to go, LET THEM GO!" and that's exactly what I'm going to do. Hell, maybe its best anyway, since he has a wife and three damn kids at home.

I closed the door after Pickle left and went to look and see how much Pickle had left me. Pickle had ten one-hundred dollar bills in a little bundle on my dresser. I guess he figured since he wasted my time, he was going to make it worth my time, and he definitely did just that with a damn thousand dollars.

I sat in my living room on the couch and before I knew it, I dozed off but I jumped up and went to knock on Jarod's bedroom door. When I didn't get an answer, I opened his door and looked around and then closed his door back, when I didn't see him. Jarod has been spending his time with someone lately. If he is, I'm happy for him. He definitely deserves some happiness.

I got up and was about to lock the front door, when two guys pushed past me, almost knocking me down to the floor. They forced their way in. The guys were wearing a hat pulled down over in their face and were wearing dark shades. The guys forced me in my bedroom so they had to know which door was my bedroom door. Since they came to the right room. The guys took the hats and removed their shades as well and I knew exactly who they were.

If I ever could pull a gun out on someone before, I wish It would've been these two. I would probably shoot them dead in their face and not think a second about it. I'm pissed that I put my gun in my nightstand after I had to check Lawrence's ass, so it's no way I would be able to get to my gun with both of them here and holding me down like this.

The one that was holding my hands down, told me to take off my clothes and then took theirs off as well. One forced himself inside me, while the other one held my arms down. I moaned out in pain but of course that didn't faze them at all because this wasn't the first time they've seen my tears and heard my moans before but it didn't do any good then and I'm sure it's not going to do any good now.

I just closed my eyes so I wouldn't have to look at them while they both were raping me over and over again. The tears kept coming out the corner of my eyes, while all I felt was pure pain the entire time. Sex is something that both parties are supposed to enjoy but not in this case. These two were raping me and they didn't care how I was feeling while they were doing it. All they were concerned about was the way they felt. They finally finished and they pulled up their clothes and looked up at me as I dried the tears that were still running down the corners of my eyes. "I swear you still got some good ass, no matter how old you get. We'll both be seeing you again really soon," One of the guys said.

One of the guys looked in his pocket and threw my money on the floor, like I was beneath him and simply wasn't worth him just handing it to me or just placing it on top of my dresser, like a decent human being. The word decent was definitely not a word I would describe either one of them.

I froze on top of my bed, until I heard the front door close first and then I ran in the living room and quickly locked the front door. I ran back in my room and looked at the money they threw on the floor and counted it. It was three thousand dollars. I guess they felt that was enough for what they both did to me. This is going to be the last time I let these two hurt me again. I'm going to put an end to this one way or the other.

CHAPTER 14

"Robert"

I couldn't get my mind off Shannon today. That girl is a damn freak. The way she sat on my desk and spread her legs wide open and then made me come close to her, just to get a sniff of it, nearly drove me wild and to top it all off, the girl then sat on my lap grinding her body on top of me, going back and forth.

Shannon is something else and I want her badly. I wanted some of her so badly that I wanted to go drag her ass back in my office after she left, leaving me with blue balls. I just wanted to have some hot ass sex, where there's nothing but just slapping ass and hard down fucking until the two of us hit that peak where we both explode together. Hell, it's been so long since I felt that kind of desire, while thinking of having sex.

That's why I wanted to do this with Shannon, because I know that damn girl is going to give me all that hot nasty sex that I want from her and I need that in my life right now. Shit, I wonder if I will be able to go tonight to get me some. I guess I'll see how this will work out.

I sat in the room and laid on the bed. Airene and I still weren't speaking to each other. She has the nerve to be walking around, like she didn't do anything wrong. I wasn't going to give her the satisfaction of going back and forth with her, about something I feel so strongly about.

Its' six-thirty, so I'm going to see if she's going to go in the kitchen to make dinner, if not, I got a backup plan. I'll just call in for a pizza and have them deliver it. I waited for a little while longer before going to see if she was cooking dinner or not. I looked up at the clock and saw it was six-forty-eight. I decided to go around in the kitchen, just to see what Airene was doing or if she was in fact trying to make dinner.

Airene was sitting in the living room playing on her phone. I wasn't going to ask her any questions or anything. I went back to my room and called in for a pizza. The young man told me he would be here in about twenty minutes.

I sat on my bed, looking at Facebook, when I heard a car door close outside. I peeked out the window and saw that the pizza delivery man was outside. I grabbed my wallet and took out a twenty-dollar bill to pay the young man. "Hello sir. Here's your pizza, the guy said, showing the pizza to me. "Thanks, enjoy your night," I said, handing the guy the twenty-dollar bill.

I went and told Robin that dinner was ready so she could get washed up and I washed my hands as well. I grabbed two paper plates and two bottles of water and sat them on the table. Robin grabbed a paper plate and got her two pieces. "How many can I get Dad?" Robin asked. "Get how many you want," I said. Robin nodded her head. I'm not concern if Airene eat or not, just as long as Robin and I ate.

I grabbed two big slices and we started eating. Robin grabbed another slice and I did as well. Robin told me how school was coming along and that she has an English test to prepare for. Robin said she was hoping to get an "A" in the class but she got a "B" on her last test. I told Robin to keep working because the teacher might drop the lowest test scores, which will put her right up there.

Robin's face lit up after I said that. She told me she didn't think of that so that was definitely a possibility. Robin and I finished eating our pizza and I left the box on top of the table in case Airene wanted any.

I decided to take a hot shower, because I have to get out of here. I threw on some jeans and a tee-shirt and put on my baseball cap and grabbed my wheat Timberland boots that Ryan got me one year for my birthday. Ryan teased me and told me he knows I'll probably never wear them but today would be my sixth time wearing them since it's just now September. He would definitely get a kick out of seeing his old man in some Timberlands.

I grabbed my phone and texted Shannon. I wanted to see if we can finish what we started today. Shannon texted back and told me to call her. I called her and waited for her to answer the phone. "Hey Robert. How are you?" Shannon asked. "I'm good and you?" I replied. "I'm okay, just laying on my couch and playing with myself," Shannon said in a seductive voice, already turning me on.

I swear there was something about Shannon that I find extremely exotic and that was turning me on way more than I care to admit. "Damn, you couldn't wait on me?" I asked. "How would I know that I would hear from you today? I thought maybe I scared you off with my little strip tease," Shannon said. "Oh hell no. If anything you turned me on the way on so what you showed me today, trust me a brother is all in," I said. "Is that right? Well, I have a place you can be all in right now if you want?" Shannon said, laughing. "Send me your address," I said. "Okay, cool," Shannon said, hanging up the phone.

I grabbed my keys off the table and was heading out the door, when I realized that I was right behind Airene. Airene turned around when she saw me behind her, locking the house door. She didn't say anything and neither did I. I think we both knew that our marriage had run its course and it was nothing worth trying to save or hold on to.

I would say it was because how she treated Ryan but I knew that wasn't just it. Airene felt like because I have a pretty good job that pays really well, she feels like I should pay all the bills and the small bills, like water bill, cable, internet, and grocery bill are the only things she should have to pay. I told her if I pay the bills like that she'll always keep money in her pocket and I'll always be broke and that's not how it's going to be. Sometimes Airene would come home from work and wouldn't attempt to try to cook or clean the house or anything, so if I don't decide on something for Robin and me to eat, we would basically starve waiting on Airene to get up off her ass and do something. When this happened with Ryan the other night was pretty much a done deal with me. I know marriage is not the easiest thing to be in and it's going to definitely take some work but I think Airene threw in the towel a long time ago and now I'm at that point that I'm throwing it in too.

I got in my car and took off. I put Shannon's address in my

GPS and headed over there. Damn, I don't have any condoms. I'll have to stop by a convenience store and get some. I went through the next three lights and spotted the 7/11 on the corner. I ran inside and grabbed a box of Magnum condoms. I looked around, hoping I didn't see anyone I know but Lord behold, I saw Deacon Samuels getting a beer from the cooler. I prayed the cashier would hurry up and ring me up, so I could get the hell out of here before Deacon Samuels sees me. Deacon Samuels is about eighty-three years old and if he saw me, he would try to talk my head off and I don't have time for that. Luckily, the young lady rung me up and I was able to pay for my condoms before Deacon Samuels even closed the cooler door for his beer.

I pulled up to a small brick house and got out of my car. I went to the door and knocked. The door opened up but I didn't see anyone. Where the hell is Shannon? I just stood in the living room, looking around but I still didn't see Shannon. I was about to go when I saw Shannon appear from around the corner, wearing a police outfit, without the pants though. She wore the police hat and had a black nightstick in her hand, along with some handcuffs around her wrist. She had her blue shirt, opened up to show off her beautiful rack that was sitting there and looking delicious. "Oh hot damn!" I said to myself knowing Shannon was about to give me an experience that I'll never forget and a brother couldn't wait.

Shannon grabbed me by the hand and took me to the back of the house in a room. The room was dark, as if the lighting was of a dim purple color or something. I started noticing some of the things that Shannon had in the room. She had all kinds of kinky shit in here, like swings and some kind of chamber and all kinds of things that had straps that looked like a table you would strap someone down to.

Shannon demanded me to take off all my clothes and then she handed me something that look like a damn dog collar and she had the chain in her hand. "Put this on Robert. Are you willing to try some freaky shit with me?" Shannon asked. "As long as it's just us and you not trying to invite other dudes in here, thinking they about to fuck me or something? Because trust me, It's definitely not that kind of party here," I said. "Okay, I can respect that," Shannon said.

Something tells me after this night with Shannon, we'll definitely no longer have that friendly manager/assistant, relationship anymore. We're about to take this shit to entirely different levels all together and my ass couldn't wait.

CHAPTER 15
"Ryan"

I only have fifteen minutes left before lunch. I think I'll eat the lunch the cafeteria workers have prepared. Bradly hasn't been back in class this morning. This is the second day he missed in my class in a row. I just hope he's alright and nothing has happened.

The bell rung and the kids ran out of class, like the building was on fire or something. I guess they must all be hungry as well. I headed to the cafeteria and saw Lawrence turning the corner in front of me. Instead of him holding the door open for me, he allowed it to shut in my face. I guess he's still a little salty about last night, when he thought he was going to manhandle me and get what he wanted, without paying me my fee upfront. I bet I had something for that ass though.

I saw that they had spaghetti, salad, garlic bread and cinnamon rolls for lunch, which was good by me. I sat down at the table and Sonia came and joined me. "Hey, what's up Sonia?" I asked. "I'm good Ryan. How are you?" Sonia asked. "I'm doing good, just ready for the day to be over with," I said. "You and me both," Sonia replied.

Sonia talked about Leon and their two children and how bad her children are. I told her about my sister and stepmother and the drama that went down earlier this week at their house. Sonia told me she knew Airene was all about drama, ever since the first time she met her. I laughed and told her she was dead on it. Sonia said she has an aunt just like Airene, so she knew exactly what to expect from her. Sonia teaches eighth grade math here at the school and attends my father's church. She's a year older than me but we've always been pretty cool growing up. She always tried to act like I'm her little brother, since she's the only child.

After lunch, I passed Ms. Smith in the hallway, as I was heading back to my class. "Mr. Ryan, you don't have a class right now do you?" Ms. Smith asked. "No I don't," I replied. "Well, can you stop by my office in about ten minutes please? I need to see you for a second," Ms. Smith said. "Okay I will," I replied. I went to my classroom and put my things up. Let me go see what this woman wants with me.

I walked down to Ms. Smith's office and knocked on the door. "Come on in," Ms. Smith said. I walked in her office and sat down at the desk. Ms. Smith looked like she was texting someone on her phone. She then put her phone up. I took my phone out of my pocket and held it in my hand. "Ms. Smith, what is it that you want?" I asked.

Ms. Smith stood up from her desk and walked toward me. "Ryan, are you gay?" Ms. Smith asked. I wasn't sure if I was hearing this woman right. Did she just ask me if I was gay? Which is definitely against school rules to ask someone about their sexual orientation, but I still wasn't sure if I heard Ms. Smith right in the first place. "Ms. Smith, can you please ask me that question again because I'm not sure if I heard you right the first time," I said. "Sure, I asked if you were gay?" Ms. Smith repeated herself. Acting like it was okay, which I'm sure she knows it's against the law to ask an employee something like that. "Maybe I am and maybe I'm not," I said, with a smile. "I sure wouldn't mind seeing for myself?" Ms. Smith said, licking her lips. "So you're trying to give me some huh?" I asked. "I sure am." Ms. Smith said, closing her blinds and getting up, locking her office door.

I just wanted to see just how far she wanted to take this. Ms. Smith told me to stand up and when I did she whipped out my penis and took it into her mouth, sucking me as if she was a vacuum cleaner or something. "Ms. Smith, are you sure we should be doing this in your office?" I asked. "Well, I am the school principal and as long as you're fine with it then I'm fine with it," Ms. Smith said.

I adjusted my phone in my hand as Ms. Smith pulled me down in the chair I was sitting in prior so I could reap the entire benefits of the free head I was receiving at work and in her office. I'm not going to lie, Ms. Smith knew exactly what she was doing by the way she was working those lips around my shaft, acting like she was sucking a lollipop or something.

It's a little surprising for a lady of her standards and position that she's doing something so slutty in her office like this, without a care in the world. "How does it feel?" Ms. Smith asked, as she looked up at me, while my penis was in her mouth and her lips were wrapped around me. "It feels great," I said, almost sounding like Tony the Tiger. I smiled as I thought about what I just thought to myself. "I guess you know what you're doing huh?" I said, laughing. "I sure would like to think I do. I bet no man can suck you like that huh?" Ms. Smith said, like I confirmed to her that I was indeed gay.

I ignored her last comment, still trying to enjoy the experience. I felt my body get that heated feeling, knowing it was time for me to release myself. "Oh damn, I'm about to, about to, about to," I said never finishing my statement and I reached that ultimate moment that no man could ever deny.

I tried to get up but Ms. Smith pushed me back down in the chair, swallowing every last drop from me as if she was afraid to not get it all or something.

I had to sit here for a few seconds, just to get myself together. I knew I couldn't move until I got right. My mind and my thoughts were all over the place. I was finally able to stand straight up and pull my pants back up as I straightened myself up. Ms. Smith was sitting at her desk, looking in her makeup compact mirror, I guess to make sure she didn't leave any evidence around her mouth or anything or her hair out of place.

I stood up, from my chair. "Is that all you have for me Ms. Smith?" I asked, trying to put my professionalism back on. "Yes that is all. I hope you enjoyed our little experience and that we could do it again soon. I still haven't come to my conclusion if you're gay or straight. I guess we'll have to keep on doing it until I know," Ms. Smith said. "Well my sexuality has nothing to do with whether you can get my dick hard by putting it in your mouth. I'm sure anyone would be able to do that, especially how good you are at it," I said, winking my eye at her and walking out of her office.

I walked back to my class, thinking of what just happened but hell if Ms. Smith wanted some of me, she could've already asked, without trying to see if I'm straight or gay. But I think that was just her way of getting what she wanted and using that as her reason.

CHAPTER 16
"Robert"

I finished my little escapade with Shannon and was on my way home. I pulled up in my driveway at the same time as Airene did. We didn't exchange any words or anything. It was basically like our bodies were here but all our love and feelings were gone for each other and I think she knew that as well.

I opened the door and held it open for her. Airene just walked on in the house without even a thank you, I shook my head and locked the front door. I gathered my things to take a hot shower and to prepare myself for bed.

I turned the water on and as it hit my face, I was able to reflect back on my life and the direction it was heading in. I knew I love Airene but I think after I found out how she really felt about Ryan, that tore at my heart and made me want to pull away from her. I know she's entitled to her own opinion but to have said what she said while he was still here, was definitely uncalled for. Then she kept saying more horrible stuff that if Ryan's not careful he's going to eventually die from Aids. Why would she say some shit like that to me?

I admit that I think Ryan is definitely out there more than I'd like to know but I'm just praying he's protecting himself. I finished drying myself off and shaving my face and head. I put on my pajamas and I knew it was time for me to have that conversation with Airene.

I went to my old bedroom door and knocked. "Come in," Airene said. I opened the door and closed it. "I thought you were Robin," Airene said, looking disappointed. "Oh okay. I won't take up much of your time. But, I think we need to talk," I said. "Okay well shoot," Airene said, looking directly at me.

I sat in the corner chair while Airene was on the bed, looking like she was ready to hear what I have to say. "Look Airene, I think our marriage has run its course and I think it's fair to say, it's over with. Now you have signed a prenuptial agreement before we got married so what's mine is mine and what's yours is yours. Now we can go ahead and get a divorce and you can find you a place and Robin, if she wants to live with you or you and her can continue living here if you're okay with that?

You can keep the master bedroom and I'll continue to sleep in Ryan's old room, that way you won't have to look for a place. You can come and go as you please, just as I'll do the same. We'll continue paying the bills like we've been paying it straight down the middle and no one is allowed to have overnight guests at our house. Wherever you stay that night is totally up to you," I said.

Airene wasn't saying anything, she was just looking at me with a deranged look on her face, as if she couldn't believe the words that were coming out of my mouth. "So you're ready to give up and throw away the towel?" Airene asked. "Yes I am, because your views are totally different from mine and It's not that we both have to share the same views on anything or everything, I just can't sit around and allow you to mistreat or degrade my son because you feel the way you do about his sexuality.

Ryan has been picked on and teased his entire life about that and for me to be his father and allow my own wife to talk and speak to him the way you did that night, will look like I don't have his back. I've always told my son, that when all his cheerleaders are gone and he doesn't hear those "well done, good job, or I'm proud of you," he will always hear it from me," I said.

Airene got up from off the bed and walked toward me. She leaned over and kissed me. "Baby, let's not throw our marriage away based on that argument we had that night. I'm sorry for what Ryan heard me say about him when he was over here. I should've never allowed him to hear me talking about him," Airene said.

I played what Airene just said to me over in my head. She said she's sorry for what Ryan heard her say and she should've never allowed him to hear her talking about him. So I guess she felt she could've said whatever she wanted to say but she shouldn't have allowed him to hear it.

I shook my head at Airene's comment because she was quite aware with how she was wording what she just said to me, she wanted to see if I caught on to it and yes I definitely did. "So you will apologize to Ryan if he comes over for what you said to him?" I asked. "I'll apologize to Ryan for what he heard me say," Airene said.

I stood and shook my head, "I'm not up for this rephrasing word games that you're playing. So yes it's better that we just keep it like how it is. So have a goodnight," I said, walking out the door and heading back to my room. I'm not going to go back and forth with Airene. She has her own views on her beliefs and I do as well.

I took off my pajamas and got in bed. I was about to go to sleep until I received a notification that came through my phone. I looked at my phone; it was a text from Shannon. "Hey big Daddy, I had fun tonight and I can't wait for the next time we get together. Maybe next time we can explore some more other wild and kinky things," Shannon said. I replied back saying "okay," then a picture came through of Shannon laying on top of a bar counter with a big dildo inside her.

I burst out laughing, not realizing that Shannon was such a huge freak like that. It's amazing how you can work with a person for so long and never really know them or certain things about them. I guess it's a good thing I never knew this about Shannon because maybe I would've ended things along time ago with Airene.

CHAPTER 17

"Ryan"

I just got to work and was ready to leave already. I wasn't able to sleep for the last two nights, since those two fools popped up on me like I have them scheduled or something. I guess they feel that I'm a part of their property since they've been doing this kind of thing for a long time.

I tried to think about something different so I wouldn't be depressed at work. I need a weekend trip to just go somewhere and relax. Dad was talking about a weekend trip with his two friends and one with just us and I think I would like that.

I had a few minutes before my class gets in. I made sure I was refreshed to start my day with them. You have to be on your game with seventh graders, especially if they catch you sleeping, which they did last week.

I saw Lawrence and Ms. Smith at my door knocking. "I know damn well Ms. Smith isn't trying to have a freaking threesome with me and Lawrence and it's not even eight-o'clock yet," I said to myself, while opening the door. Lawrence and Ms. Smith had a worried look on their face, like someone had died or something. "Why you two looking like that?" I asked. "Because we have some serious allegations that we have to discuss with you. Please come with us," Lawrence said.

I walked to Ms. Smith's office and Lawrence closed the door behind us. I sat down, ready to know what the hell is going on this morning. "Ryan, one of your students came forth and said that you touched him in an inappropriate place," Ms. Smith said. "What!" I yelled. "Yes. When I got here this morning it was on my voicemail. Ryan, because I'm the principal and you're a teacher, I'm supposed to call the police and have them escort you off the premises. CPS is already investigating it, as well as Sled. So what I'm going to do is allow you to go ahead up to the police station to give your statement.

You're under administrative leave without pay until your investigation clears you. When your investigation is over, you will get paid for each day that you missed work. Do you have any questions for me?" Ms. Smith asked. "No I don't, but this isn't right. I would never do anything like that to a child or a student," I said. "I know Ryan. I know you didn't do this but it's out of my hands," Ms. Smith said. "You need to make this go away," I said. "I'm sorry Ryan, there is nothing I can do. Now I can give you an hour to be at the police station before they come looking for you," Ms. Smith said. "I'm on my way up there now," I said. "Good." Ms. Smith said.

Lawrence grabbed my things before we left my classroom so he handed them to me. "I'm really sorry this is happening to you," Lawrence said. "Thank you," I replied.

I left the school and headed over to the police station. I called my dad and told him what was going on and that I was on my way to the police station. Dad was furious that the police would even think I would do something like that. I had to remind Dad, that the police didn't know me and I guess to them there was no telling if I did or didn't do what I'm being accused of. They have to take all allegations seriously because I could have been a child molester or a pedophile that would do something like that to a child. Dad told me that was definitely true but he knows that I'm not capable of doing anything like that. That's one thing about knowing a person's character; there are certain things you know without a doubt in your mind that they wouldn't do what they're being accused of and my Dad knows I would never do something like that.

I hung up the phone with Dad and walked into the police station. I told them who I was and two officers immediately came from the back to arrest me. They read me my rights and put the handcuffs on me. They took all my things and put them inside a big zip-lock bag. They made me take my mugshots and fingerprinted me. They walked me down to a cell and the officer pushed me inside, as if I were a wild animal that was a threat to other people. I sat on the bench, feeling like a real animal behind bars and there was nothing I could do about the lies that got me here in the first place.

My father told me that hopefully he would be able to get me out of this mess as quickly as possible. The police said that my trial should be set probably by tomorrow morning. I sat inside the jail cell with three other guys. I swear if you're not a tough ass guy, this place is definitely not for the weak. Shit, who am I fooling? Where the hell am I tough at? There's only three other inmates in here and they're looking at me like I'm a piece of raw steak, that was just thrown to a bunch of wolves and they're about to devour me.

I'm so ready to get out of here, that I'm about to lose it. I called one of my frat brothers, Cornelius Rogers, that's a defense attorney to see if he could help me out. Cornelius told me not to worry about anything; that he was on the case now.

Cornelius told me I should be out no later than tomorrow morning, so to hang tight. I wanted to ask Cornelius where the hell was I going, to another damn corner to sit on a different bench or something. I thanked Cornelius for helping me and he told me he would be at my hearing first thing in the morning.

I'm surprised Cornelius is willing to help me, since we were never friends in college. We're both a part of the same fraternity and would occasionally hold conversations from time to time. I guess he knew deep down that I could never do anything like that to a child so I guess that's why he's willing to helping me. I sat on my jail bunk trying to think how the hell I got here. This shit is so damn unfair! I didn't do anything to Bradly and he knows that. Why the hell Is he lying on me?

This dark-skinned dude with big muscles came and sat beside me on my bunk. "What's up? What you in here for?" the guy asked. I was about to tell him the truth, that I'm accused of inappropriate behavior with a child, but I remember when my Dad's uncle always said there's two things that an inmate will slice your throat for, if they find out that you killed or molested a child, so I had to think of something else really quick to say. "I took a car that I rented and kept it way longer than I was supposed to so they got me on car theft," I said. "Dang, how long were you supposed to keep the car?" the guy asked. "Just for the weekend," I said. "Well how long did you end up keeping it?" he asked. "Three months," I said. "Damn man, that's some gangster type shit there. I guess you say you wasn't giving up that ride huh?" the guy said, laughing.

I cracked a smile at the guy and then I started laughing. I guess he definitely couldn't see me doing that kind of shit. "Man, what I thought you did was nothing like what you actually did," the guy said. "What did you think I did?" I asked. "I thought you probably got caught getting fucked behind a building or in an alley or something," the guy said. I almost choked on my own saliva when he said that. Who the hell does he think I am, some damn teenage boy that would just do it any damn where and with any damn body. I knew I had to do something crazy because if I didn't, this dude and the other two were probably going to fuck with me, while I try to sleep tonight.

I knew exactly what I was going to do to make damn sure these motherfuckers wouldn't try to murder me in my sleep or gang rape me or something. The guy was still trying to make small talk with me and I started laughing. I mean laughing my damn ass off, like I was losing my damn mind and was on the verge of being suicidal type shit. I wanted these fools to think I was a sociopath and would bite their dicks off if they came anywhere near me. That big ass dude jumped up so fast off my bed and ran in the damn corner, like I was the big bad wolf and I was coming to get his milk and cookies.

I ran over there near the muscular dude, hitting my chest as if I was Tarzan and roaring like I was a fucking lion. I was drooling out of the mouth and acting like I lost my damn mind as I ran over there toward him. I jumped at the dude and when he jumped back, he lost control and busted his ass on the floor. He got up yelling and pointing. "Guard! Guard!" the muscular dude yelled.

Two guards ran towards our cell. "What the hell is going on in there!" the guard yelled. "That motherfucker is crazy!" the dude said, backing up from me. "I ain't crazy! That fucker tried to rape me!" I yelled, still drooling from the mouth. "I ain't tried to rape your crazy, fool ass!" the man said, still looking scared. "Alright, settle down in there. If I have to come back down this damn hall one more fucking time, I swear neither one of you are going to like it! So Randal, get your ass over in this bunk and your crazy ass get over there in that bunk! And don't let me have to come down here again!" the guard said, walking off.

I walked back towards my bunk but before I did, I jumped toward the muscular guy and he jumped back so damn fast, I know he probably got whiplash. The other two inmates were looking scared as hell, not knowing what I was capable of. I smiled to myself as I walked back to my bunk. I bet I showed these motherfuckers crazy, I guess I don't have to worry about them coming anywhere close to my bunk tonight while I'm asleep. Sometimes you just have to go against your own fears and show that you'll fight If you have to and at this point, I'm just fighting for survival just to get through this damn night.

I laid down on this nasty ass bottom bunk, trying to think where this damn lie came from. I knew it was Bradly but what I can't figure out is why would he lie and say I touched him when he knew damn well I didn't. I'm sure that damn Lawrence is behind this shit. It has his name written all over it since I refused to have sex with him and pulled out a gun. This fool is trying to get revenge on me. I think I'm right but if I am, that fool won't know what revenge is when I get done with him.

I tried to get some sleep but it was definitely hard, every time I looked around that damn muscular dude was looking at me. I sure hope his dumb looking ass doesn't try anything, even though I know I can't fight him off but If I have to scream like a little girl, until I wake up everybody that lives around this jail, believe me I will. I kept my back against the wall just praying that no one would touch me and I can just make it through the night.

I finally was able to get some sleep but I kept waking up every hour to make sure that everyone was right where their ass is supposed to be and not standing over me with their dick over my face jacking off and smiling. That shit will definitely freak me the hell out.

I closed my eyes again, and within minutes I was in a deep sleep. My mind had me drifting off to a place that was familiar to me. I was in my bedroom at home, sleeping in my own bed. I felt a warm touch against my face, I opened my eyes and it was my mother. "Hey son. How are you?" Mom asked. "Mom, I'm okay but is that really you?" I asked. "Yes son, the one and only," Mom said.

Mom looked exactly how I remembered her. Mom still had her long, black, beautiful hair and brown, silky complexion. It was definitely my mom. "Mom, what are you doing here in my dream?" I asked. "Because I wanted you to see your life and what's in store for you if you don't change your ways. Ryan, son you're doing too much and enough is enough now. Baby, God is trying to tell you something and you're still not listening but you better start listening. Sometimes, it takes something like this to happen just for you to change and realize the way you're living is not of God. You're playing a dangerous game with all this escorting and sleeping around with all these different men. Please stop son before it's too late," Mom said. "Mom, I'll stop. I don't want to end up dying," I said. "Good baby. Your father and your sister love you and I want you to be around for them. So please try to live your life right baby and let that escorting mess go," Mom said.

I jumped up from out of my sleep and stood up, thinking about the dream I just had. It was the first dream I had about Mom in the last five years. Mom had a mission that she knew she needed to talk to me about and I know I have to stop living my life like this. I don't want to end up dying because some John Doe ended up killing me because I didn't do something right, or they decided they weren't gay and took their denial and frustration out on me and took it to the extreme. Yes, I know when to throw in the towel and let it go and that's exactly what I'm prepared to do. "Thank you Mom, for still looking down on me," I said, trying to go back to sleep.

CHAPTER 18
"Robert"

I went to Ryan's bail hearing and the judge let Ryan off on a twenty-five-thousand-dollar bail judgment. Thank God I only had to pay ten percent of that. I'm glad I took off the entire day to spend with Ryan. The judge has set Ryan's court day for a month from now.

Ryan was so upset that he wouldn't be able to pay his bills due to being out of work and he couldn't go back until he was cleared of all charges. I told Ryan to not worry about that because I'll take care of everything until he can go back to work but I had to make sure that Ryan didn't do what he's being accused of so I asked him.

Ryan looked me dead in the face and straight in the eye and told me that he didn't do that and he has no idea why someone would target him for a crime as vicious as that, that could mess up his entire life as well as his career. I told Ryan I don't know who would do that but it doesn't take much for someone to dislike you for no reason. People can dislike you just because of the confidence you carry about yourself of being good looking, being smart, or just seems like you have everything going good for yourself. It just doesn't take much for people to want to see you down to their level.

Ryan sat on the passenger side, listening to me as I tried talking to him, about life and the direction he sees himself going. I even told him that I'm aware of him sleeping with all these men and that he needs to stop doing that. Ryan was shocked, wondering how I knew. I told Ryan that it's all over the internet of his little website he has up. "Young man looking for a Sugar Daddy to take care of him. If you got the cash, then I give up the ass." Ryan looked shocked, but I told him if it was that easy for someone to pull up his website to show me, then it would be easy for someone else like an employer or one of his students' parents to do the same exact thing. I wanted to shake some damn sense into Ryan and I asked him what the hell he was thinking, knowing what he does for a living to do something so damn stupid. Ryan told me that was true and for me not to worry because he's going to turn over a new leaf and start living and doing right.

For once I believed Ryan will actually do that. It was the same look that he used to have in his eyes when he tried his best to do something that he never thought he could do and eventually does it and excels in it. I have a feeling that Ryan is now going to be okay. I think it took something like this to happen, just for Ryan to realize his lifestyle wasn't doing it for him and he needed a change. I think the change is now.

Ryan and I said we were going to take a little trip somewhere but I didn't think it would be this soon and on a weekday, but sometimes things don't always work out or go according to plan like we would like it to.

Ryan was knocked out on the passenger side, sound asleep. I just smiled at the image of him as if he was still thirteen or fourteen years old and I would take him to his track meets or basketball games, while he would be sound asleep on the passenger side.

Those were some of the proudest and happiest times I had with my son. Now Ryan is all grown up and living his own life and it seems he barely has time for his old man anymore, but that's when God throws that monkey wrench in your plans and you end up backtracking a little bit.

I parked the car and Ryan finally woke up. "So I guess we're here huh?" Ryan asked. "Yes sir, we're here. You woke up just in time," I said. "I see," Ryan replied. "Help me get the lawn chairs out the trunk," I said. "Okay," Ryan replied, grabbing the chairs and the cooler while I grabbed the tent. We set everything up on the beach and then sat under the tent. I looked over at Ryan and he looked peaceful, but I could tell he still had a lot on his mind. "Are you okay son?" I asked. "Yeah, I'll be okay Dad. I had a dream about Mom last night," Ryan said. "Oh really? Do you want to share it with me?" I asked.

Ryan adjusted his lawn chair and put his sunglasses on. "She told me I was doing too much and it was time for me to change before something happens to me," Ryan said. "Wow, that sounds like some good advice to me son, and I can't help but to agree with her. You're doing entirely too much and it's time for you to slow your role.

Just because you can do something Ryan, doesn't mean you should do it. Choices always brings consequences. Some can be good and some can be bad but you have to make sure that the choices you make are right for you. You're not going to always have me to be able to fall back on. One of these days I won't be here son. I just want you to make good decisions, that's all," I said. "You're right Dad. I'm going to get myself together," Ryan said.

I think Ryan needed this to happen to him in order for him to see how he's living his life, that eventually things come to an end. I don't think Ryan touched that student in an inappropriate way but I think he needed this to happen in order for him to take a step back and just look at his life and the attention he is causing by what all he's doing. Maybe now he'll start trying to change and get his life back on track.

Ryan got up to stretch his arms and legs. "Dad, how are things with you and Airene? I hope she isn't still mad with me?" Ryan asked. "Why would she be upset with you?" I asked. "I don't know, I guess because she doesn't like how I'm living my life," Ryan said. "Well, she doesn't have a say so in that. We're basically separated. I'm sleeping in your old room and she's in our room," I said.

Ryan looked shocked when I told him that. "So you two do whatever you want to do?" Ryan asked. "Yes, we just can't bring anyone back home with us so whoever we decide to be with, that's just that," I said. "Wow, I couldn't go for that while they're living in my house," Ryan said. "Well when you get to be our age, and you don't want to start over, that's what a lot of couples are doing these days," I said.

I'm sure Ryan has a lot of questions of trying to understand why Airene and I are now living this way but that's all he's getting for now. I would never tell him that Airene and I just couldn't come to an understanding about his lifestyle. I definitely didn't want to make him feel like any of this was his fault and make him feel any worse than how he's already feeling but I think he already knows that Airene can't accept him and calling him out his name was the straw that broke the camel's back for me.

Ryan and I had a great time at the beach. We ate, swam a little, did a lot of talking and male bonding and he told me what he's planning on doing in the future. I'm pleasantly surprised that Ryan wants to open up a youth center for all the youth to help them stay out of trouble and keep them off the street. I think when all this is over with, maybe I'll help Ryan get his business idea started, if he's still serious about it. I guess time will tell if he is or not.

CHAPTER 19
"Ryan"

Today was the day of my trial. Cornelius asked me to take some pictures of my townhouse, in the living room, kitchen, bathroom and bedroom as well. He told me he needed a lot and in different angles and all. I wanted to ask him why but I didn't ask any questions about it, I just did what he asked. I know Cornelius has a pretty impressive winning record for all the people he's gotten off so I figured it would be easy for him to get me off since I'm not guilty of what I'm being accused of.

I grabbed my keys off the table and headed out the door. My Dad told me he would be at my trial every step of the way, if it's a continuation or just a one-day trial, he would be there to support me, which I knew he would.

I pulled up in the parking lot and just sat and waited for a few minutes to just talk and pray to God. I asked God to allow the truth to come out so I can be free from these allegations that are sitting over my head right now. I just hope God hears a sinner's prayer because after this trial is over with, I'm definitely going to make some positive changes in my life, putting my escorting days behind me. I have a feeling if I keep doing that, I'll catch something or end up getting killed.

I walked into the courthouse and they checked me in and told me my trial isn't until nine-thirty. I looked at my watch and saw it was only eight-twenty. I have over an hour to kill which is a good thing. I'd rather be early than running late any day.

I decided to go to the cafeteria here to get a little breakfast, since I didn't eat anything this morning before I left my house. I felt my phone vibrate in my pocket. I looked at it and saw that Dad texted me and told me he just pulled up. I told him I was in the cafeteria about to get something to eat. He told me he was walking up now.

I decided on a little cheese Danish, a banana, and a cup of coffee. That will at least hold me until lunch time. Dad finally walked in. "Hey son," Dad said, as he hugged me tightly. "Hey Dad," I said, as we both sat down at the table. Dad got a banana and some coffee as well.

We talked a little bit until it was time for us to head to the courtroom for the trial. "Ryan are you ready? It's time," Dad said. "As ready as I'm going to be," I said. "Okay, I know you're a bit nervous but I'm sure that everything will go in your favor son. You didn't do anything wrong so hopefully Cornelius will be able to prove that." Dad said. "I sure hope so," I replied.

Dad and I met Cornelius at the door. "Good morning Mr. Jacobs, and it's good to see you again Ryan," Cornelius said, as he shook our hands. Dad walked on inside and took a seat. Cornelius looked much different dressed up in a suit but I guess he probably said the same thing about me. "Are you ready to do this Ryan?" Cornelius asked. "I am. Are you confident we can win this case?" I asked. "I certainly am. I found out a lot of interesting things, I just have to see how it's going to unfold," Cornelius said.

Cornelius sounded very confident like he got this case right where he wants it, which I definitely hope so because I can't go to damn prison for something I didn't do. Cornelius and I walked inside and I took my seat beside him. The prosecutor is a tall, older, brown-skinned man. The man looks like he's been a lawyer for a long time. Cornelius has only been practicing law for four years so I just hope he knows what the hell he's doing and gets me off this bogus charge.

The judge came in and asked the lawyers to begin their opening statements. After Mr. Brown gave his opening statement which was very good, Cornelius came up to do his. It should be interesting to see what Cornelius is going to say.

Cornelius drank some water before he started talking. "Ladies and gentleman, I know the prosecutor painted you a picture of my client, which is his job to do so but he doesn't know one thing about my client. My client is Mr. Ryan Jacobs and he's been working at Webb Middle School for eight years now. He's never been written up in all the eight years that he's been there. My client is a member of the LGBTQ community, which Mr. Brown brought up in his opening statement, which I guess is relevant since that's what he's being accused of, doing something inappropriate in that nature. But that's his lifestyle and we will not judge him for that. Your job jury is to determine whether or not he did this hideous crime that he's accused of and that's it. Nothing else about who he associates with, or who he sleeps with, that's none of your business, that's none of my business, and that's certainly none of Mr. Brown's business. We must stick to the reason he's on trial, which is whether or not he did what he's being accused of, so If he did this, then yes he should be locked up under the jail and the key should be thrown away. Remember just because someone has been brought up on charges doesn't mean they're guilty. So before this case is over with, I will prove who is really behind this entire thing," Cornelius said, as he took his seat.

Cornelius' opening statement was on point. I wonder what he found out that has him so confident that we're going to win. I'm sure all that is going to be revealed. "Mr. Brown, please call your first witness," the judge said. "Your honor, I call Bradly James to the stand," Mr. Brown said.

Bradly came to the stand and the bailiff swore him in as Bradly took his seat. "Good morning Bradly," Mr. Brown said. "Good morning Bradly replied. "Look Bradly, I'm not going to be too long with you but how long have you known Mr. Jacobs?" Mr. Brown asked. "I've known him since this school year, when I got him as my science teacher. "Bradly said. "Is he fairly nice to you or is he mean to you?" Mr. Brown asked. "He's pretty nice. I've never had any problems with him," Bradly said. "Okay well tell me why you ran out of his class that day?" Mr. Brown asked. "Because he's been touching me and trying to make me do things with him that I don't want to do." Bradly said. "And that's why you got so upset and walked out of his class?" Mr. Brown asked. "Yes that's why," Bradly said.

Cornelius started jotting a lot of information down on a notepad, of what Bradly was saying as his response. I guess he needed to make sure he had his facts right when he questions Bradly. "Bradly tell us where and when did this touching take place when Mr. Jacobs did this to you?" Mr. Brown said. "He did it at his place," Bradly said. "Okay how did you get to his place?" Mr. Brown asked. "Mr. Jacobs saw me walking home from school one day and he asked If I needed a ride and I told him yes. He picked me up and told me he would take me home but he had to get something out of his place first so he brought me to his house, and that's when he started touching me and doing other things to me." Bradly said. "Okay well, can you describe his place for us?" Mr. Brown asked. "His couch is dark brown, and he has a big brown and beige rug under the coffee table in his living room. His curtains are brown and beige and his coffee table and end tables are a dark walnut color. He also has a picture of rocks and vases and it's in a brown picture frame on his living room wall." Bradly said.

My mouth dropped because how in the world did Bradly know this, especially since he's never been to my house before. Someone is definitely behind this but who in the world. I know Cornelius is about to get to the damn truth and it's only a matter of time before all this comes out, especially since he's been to my townhouse before to know exactly how it looks and the décor of my house. I guess that's the reason why he wanted me to take all those pictures of my house so he can have the proof he needs. "Your honor, I don't have any more questions for Mr. James right now," Mr. Brown said.

Cornelius stood up and walked towards Bradly. "Bradly, how are you doing this morning?" Cornelius asked. "I'm doing good," Bradly said. "Good Bradly. I want to ask you this question first," Cornelius said. "Okay, Bradly replied. "Bradly, are you aware what the truth is from a lie?" Cornelius asked. "Yes, I know the difference," Bradly said. "Okay I'm glad you do, but I'm a little confused, since this is only like the third week in September and you just went back to school the last week in August but yet you ended up going to Mr. Jacobs house?" Cornelius asked. "Well he saw me walking from school and he asked if I needed a ride and he gave me a ride but he brought me to his house first," Bradly said, looking nervous and was starting to sweat.

I could tell that someone had coached Bradly to say these things that he's saying but who would do that? Cornelius is about to bring it in for the kill. "Bradly, you described Mr. Jacobs house exactly how it used to look three years ago. So three years ago you would've been in the fourth grade and only 9years old. Your Honor, I would like to use this as evidence "A", which is a Badcock furniture receipt when Mr. Jacobs had gotten brand new furniture in March of 2021, which he's still paying on until this day. So Bradly, how in the world can you describe how Mr. Jacobs house looked over three years ago, if you never knew him then and Mr. Jacobs now has brand new furniture since then?

I can tell you how he knows that because Mr. Bradly was coached and told how Mr. Jacobs house looked but the only thing about that is, whoever told Bradly that didn't know that Mr. Jacobs got new furniture. Your Honor, I have pictures of Mr. Jacobs entire house from certain angles, plus I have seen it as well and I'm willing to call Mr. Jacobs current roommate up as a witness to testify on how their house looks now. So Bradly, please tell us the truth since you said earlier that you know the difference from the truth and a lie, so I'm going to ask you again, have you ever been to Mr. Jacobs house?" Cornelius asked Bradly.

Bradly knew his lies were falling apart and Cornelius had him exactly where he wanted him. "No I haven't," Bradly said, dropping his head. "Okay so who put you up to telling these lies on Mr. Jacobs? Who coached you into doing this? And Bradly, you are under oath and I've already caught you in two lies so please tell the truth before you dig yourself further and further in the ditch, you're already digging for yourself and I don't think you want to go to jail for telling more lies in court do you?" Cornelius asked. "No sir, I don't. I'll tell the truth now," Bradly said.

I guess we're all about to find out the truth of who put Bradly up to lie. "Bradly, who told you to lie on Mr. Jacobs and say that he touched you and you were at his house?" Cornelius asked. "My mom told me to say that," Bradly said. "And why would your mom tell you to say that?" Cornelius asked. "Because this lady came and offered my Mom and me money if we were to make up those lies on Mr. Jacobs. The woman wanted him to get fired because she said he is gay and he shouldn't be working with children at a school," Bradly said. "Bradly do you see the woman in the courtroom that came and talked to your mom?" Cornelius asked. "That woman right there," Bradly said pointing at someone behind me in the courtroom.

I turned around to see who Bradly was pointing at and my heart nearly jumped out of my chest when Bradly pointed at my stepmother Airene. "Bradly, what does she have on just so we can be clear who he's talking about," Cornelius said. "She has on a blue and a white striped dress," Bradly said. It was indeed Airene who had that dress on.

My father turned about five different shades when he realized that his own wife was the one behind all this. This chick hated me this bad, that she wanted me to lose my job and go to prison for something I didn't do? I swear family definitely are the ones you need to be watching, even though Airene is only my stepmother but she's married to my dad and is the one that would rather see me rotting behind prison than to be in a classroom working around children. Who the hell needs enemies if your own family are the ones putting that knife right in your back in the first place.

CHAPTER 20

"Robert"

There's no way in the world that little boy just pointed out Airene, saying that she and his mom were the ones that told him to say that Ryan brought him to his house and touched him.

Cornelius turned back around to Bradly who was still on the witness stand. "Bradly are you sure about this? Why would she ask you all to lie?" Cornelius asked. "The woman told my mom that Mr. Jacobs was gay and that he didn't need to be working around children so she needs to do what she has to do to get him fired. She then reached in her pocket and gave my mom two thousand dollars for us to say that Mr. Jacobs touched me and she gave me a one-hundred dollar bill.

I knew it was wrong and my mother knew it was wrong too but we were behind on our rent and this was two thousand dollars that was going to help us out so we had to do what we had to do in order to keep a roof over our head," Bradly said.

Everyone had a shocked look on their faces, including the judge. "Wait Bradly, I'm confused, how did Mrs. Jacobs, the lady you pointed out, know that you and your mother had an issue with Mr. Jacobs and why were you upset with Mr. Jacobs in the first place?" Cornelius asked. Bradly took a deep breath and he started wiping his eyes, as he continued. "Mr. Jacobs and I got into it because he asked me to read two paragraphs out loud in my Science book and I didn't want to because I can't read. I got upset and walked out of the class. I told my mom what happened and she was upset and we went down to the school. My mom demanded that Mr. Jacobs should get fired because of how he humiliated me. Ms. Smith told my mom that, that wasn't grounds for Mr. Jacobs to get fired because he asked everyone to read and he wasn't just singling me out, and she doubted if Mr. Jacobs knew I couldn't read because he wouldn't do anything like that.

My mom and I left the school and she was still pissed. About two days later when I got home from school, Mrs. Jacobs came to our house to talk to my mom and that's when she told my mom that Ms. Smith had told her what went down with me and Mr. Jacobs and if she wanted Mr. Jacobs fired, she had to convince us to lie on Mr. Jacobs and say that he touched me and brought me over to his house. That's when Mrs. Jacobs pulled out the envelope full of money and handed it to my mom. My mom and Mrs. Jacobs explained everything to me and told me what I needed to do and then Mrs. Jacobs handed me one-hundred dollars just for me to do what she needed me to do.

Mr. Jacobs didn't do anything to me but try to help me. My mother let money get the best of her and I let her talk me into doing a horrible thing to get Mr. Jacobs fired. I had no idea he was going to go to jail. I just thought he was going to get fired and that was it. Mr. Jacobs, please forgive me. I know what we've done to you was a terrible thing to do but we just needed the money," Bradly said. "Well Bradly, I'm glad you finally did the right thing and told the truth but that's what happens when you make up stuff on someone, you never know just how much damage that lie can really cause. Mr. Jacobs could've been in prison for a crime he didn't commit because you and three other people decided to lie on him." Cornelius said.

Cornelius turned and looked at the judge. "Your Honor, due to all this new information we just discovered, I asked that all charges be dropped against my client," Cornelius said. "I second that," Mr. Brown replied.

"Mr. Jacobs, please stand up," the judge asked. Ryan did what the judge asked and stood up. "Mr. Jacobs, on the behalf of myself and this entire courtroom, I would like to apologize for everything you went through. This was really a shame what you went through, to be lied on by one of your students and to have your stepmother, your principal and this young man's mother all play a part in this conspiracy for getting you fired and for filing false allegations, as they all played a part in all of this is absolutely horrible and I promise you they will not go unpunished for this. Officers, please arrest Mrs. Jacobs and Ms. James and I'll send out a bench warrant for Ms. Smith's arrest today as well. Again Mr. Jacobs, I'm so sorry this has happened to you but rest assured that every person that set this up will be prosecuted, today. Mr. Jacobs you are free to go with the court's apologies. The court is now adjourned," the judge said as he slammed down his gavel.

I went over to Ryan and hugged him. "Look at God son," I said. "I know Dad. I knew Airene didn't care for me but I had no idea that she hated me that much to set all this up just so I could lose my job. I mean she did a lot, even got my student, his mom and Ms. Smith involved as well. Dad, your wife needs some serious help and I hope she really gets it," I said. "Trust me son, by the time I'm done, she won't be my wife anymore, because I'm done," I said, shaking my head.

I swear it just goes to show you that you can be married to someone for so long and still not really know them, which is the case with Airene. Thirteen long years of marriage and I feel like I didn't know her at all.

Airene risked doing all that just so she could hurt my son. Someone that she knew means the world to me, but she didn't give a damn about that. All Airene cared about was hurting Ryan and hurting me as well, because she knew as long as she tried to hurt Ryan then she was hurting me too.

I know this is going to really affect Robin but I hope Airene's ass burns in hell and rots in prison, where she belongs. Anger and hurt can really tear a person down and I see it's done that to all these people that did everything to hurt Ryan. May God have mercy on each of their souls, because they're definitely going to need it.

CHAPTER 21
"Ryan"

I couldn't help from thanking Cornelius for everything he's done for me. I invited him out for dinner tonight, which he gladly accepted my invitation. Cornelius didn't charge me anything to take my case, I guess since we're fraternity brothers. My dad offered to pay him as well but he still refused any form of payment. He said he did my case pro bono and he was glad he could help. I'm just glad that all this is over with.

Lawrence texted me and told me that the police just arrested Ms. Smith about thirty minutes ago and the bell just rung so everyone saw when they brought her out in handcuffs. Lawrence said the timing was perfect and everyone was able to witness the lying manipulative woman that Ms. Smith really is.

The school board called me this afternoon and told me I can come back to work tomorrow and for everything I went through they're going to increase my pay by ten thousand dollars and write me out a check. That will definitely help with a lot of things, especially since I gave up escorting for good.

I can't believe how all this turned out in the end. It's crazy that my stepmother hated me this much, that she set all this up with Ms. Smith's help as well. It amazes me what people will do if they see you with a position or a job that they don't think you deserve.

I hope some big Shirley in prison makes Airene, Ms. Smith and Ms. James their little bitch and have them climbing the damn walls at night. I do feel sorry for Robin, having to grow up without her mother, because she wanted to see me suffer, more than being a mother to her own daughter and being there for her. I hope Bradly will be okay as well. He played a part in all this as well but I don't blame him at all. He was just following his mom, Ms. Smith and

Airene's instructions on how to get me out the door. It's amazing when someone dangles a little bit of money over someone's head, what they will do for it.

I jumped in the shower and got ready. You would think I was going on a date or something by the way I was acting. I got damn butterflies in my stomach and shit. "Come on Ryan, it's only Cornelius. Someone you've known for over twelve years, since my college days at UNC. So why am I acting like I'm actually going on a real date with him?" I said out loud, as if someone was actually there to give me a response.

I just took out my loafers and put those on. Cornelius and I haven't discussed the attire for tonight but I hope he would know to wear something casual. Cornelius is a lawyer so I wouldn't be surprised if he has on a three-piece suit.

I looked myself over one last time in the mirror before I came in the living room to watch some TV, since I have a few minutes to kill before I meet Cornelius at the restaurant. I looked up at the doorknob as the lock started to turn.

It was Jarod coming through the door. "Hey man. How are you doing?" Jarod asked as he ran up to me and hugged me tightly. "I'm doing good," I said. "I heard about your trial. I wanted to be there but I couldn't afford to be out of work," Jarod said. "Oh no, I totally understand. Everything was good." I said. "So I guess everything is okay right?" Jarod said. "Yes, everything is good. I can't believe my witch of a stepmother was behind this entire thing. She set all this up just to get me fired. Like the saying goes, "when you try to dig a hole for someone else, you better dig one for yourself as well, because you might fall right in there yourself, or something like that," I said, laughing. "Well, I know what you mean," Jarod said.

I got up to grab my keys and head out the door. "Where are you going, looking so nice?" Jarod asked. "I'm going to take Cornelius out to dinner to celebrate, plus it's my way of saying thank you for him winning my case and not charging me anything," I said. "Oh wow, he did it for free?" Jarod asked. "Yes," I replied. "Oh that was nice of him," Jarod said. "Yes it was. I probably wouldn't be a free man if Cornelius didn't figure out the majority of everything," I said. "Okay, I got you. Well you two enjoy your night," Jarod said.

I locked the door behind me as I got in my car and backed out. As I was driving, I thought about what Cornelius said in court that he was prepared to call my roommate up to testify if he needed to about our house, and the furniture but how could he do that if Jarod wasn't even at court. I guess no one knew that but him. I guess he wanted Bradly to sweat a little, which he certainly did and that's when the truth started coming out. I texted Cornelius and told him I will be there in fifteen minutes. As soon as I started driving it started pouring down rain. I hate driving in the rain. I'm just glad the restaurant is only fifteen minutes from my house. Luckily Cornelius and I pulled up at the exact same time. I parked my car beside his hunter green Mercedes and got out of the car. Cornelius came to my car door, waiting for me to get out since he had an umbrella in his hand. "What up man. Thanks for the umbrella walk," I said laughing at Cornelius.

Cornelius laughed as well, showing a very nice smile. He looked extremely handsome in his mock neck tan sweater and black jeans. His brown blazer pulled the outfit together quite nicely. "Don't you look handsome," I said. "You do as well," Cornelius said, as we walked inside.

I told the young lady that I have a reservation for Mr. Jacobs and Mr. Ross. The hostess looked on the list and told the waitress to show us to our table. We sat down at our table, which was quite nice in the corner of the restaurant.

I could tell Cornelius was extremely nervous and shy because every time I looked in his direction to say something, he was already looking at me smiling. It kind of made me a little nervous but I was okay since I knew Cornelius didn't mean anything from it.

We gave our server our food and drink order, while we sat and engaged in conversation. "You know Ryan, I can't believe I'm out on a date with you?" Cornelius said. "Oh we're on a date huh?" I asked, stretching my eyes at him. "I would like to say so," Cornelius replied. "Well, a date it is. And why can't you believe it?" I asked.

"Because I always wanted to take you out, I just didn't know how to ask you and I didn't know if you liked me like that," Cornelius said.

I just smiled at his comment because I never knew that he liked me. "I always thought you were into white guys. I didn't think you like black guys," I said. "Well to respond to your statement, I always loved African American brothers, they just were never into me. Maybe they felt like I wasn't black enough or something, or like some people like to say, that I act too white for them," Cornelius said.

I could tell that was always an issue for Cornelius, that our own race didn't accept him as if he was an outsider, trying to be black. It's so sad that sometimes our own race are the ones we're seeking approval from.

"Cornelius, I never knew that you liked me though. I actually thought you couldn't stand me, judging by the way you used to look at me," I said. "I guess that was a way for me to protect myself if I thought you would've rejected me from the start. I should've at least shoot my shot with you and I'm sure you didn't see me like that either, but at least I would be able to say I tried," Cornelius said.

I nodded my head, just as the server brought us our food and drinks. Cornelius and I ate and enjoyed good conversation with each other. He was really a nice and funny guy and he made me laugh the entire time. I'm mad at myself for not seeing that in him sooner and maybe I wouldn't have had so much bad luck in the love department with these other men, when all they wanted was just my body and not me. Who knows where Cornelius and I would've been by now and what we would've accomplished together. A power couple.

After we ate dinner, we both ordered a drink and just enjoyed each other's conversations and jokes. I was really enjoying myself. Who knew Cornelius was so damn funny, he definitely had me laughing the entire time.

The server brought the check and I quickly grabbed it to pay for it. "Now you know you really don't have to pay for my meal.

I'm more than willing to pay for the check?" Cornelius said. "Please Cornelius, you refused to let me pay your legal fees for you representing me so this is my treat to you and my way of saying thank you for everything," I said. "You're so welcome," Cornelius said with a smile.

I paid everything and as we were about to head to our cars, I turned to Cornelius as he stopped in his tracks to look at me. "I really had a great time tonight. If you want to go out again, please let me know," I said. "I want to go out again," Cornelius said, laughing. "Damn, that was quick," I said, laughing. "Well if you know what you want, there's no need to beat around the bush," Cornelius said, smiling. I dropped my head for a second and smiled. This felt so right to me and I didn't know really how to handle it. "How about tomorrow night? Maybe we can check out a movie or go bowling or something?" Cornelius said. "I would like that," I replied. "So it's a date?" Cornelius asked. "Yes it is," I said as we both got in our cars and drove off.

I can't believe I had such a great time with Cornelius. He's definitely different than I expected a date with him would be like. I will definitely hang out with him again. I actually can't wait until Saturday night for our second date. Maybe this is the start of something different for me, because my escorting days are over for good and I'm moving on to bigger and better things.

CHAPTER 22
"Robert"

I sat Robin down last night and told her what her mother did and how she's responsible for Ryan being put on administrative leave and going to jail. Robin said she doesn't know why her mother is so cruel but she said she loves her, but she thinks a few years in prison will teach her a lesson, that even she isn't above the law and the rules still apply to her.

I told Robin that was definitely true and she was really taking this better than I was expecting. Robin said there was no need to be crying over something she knew she couldn't change. She wasn't the one who lied and tried to frame her brother. Robin said that her mother just has to learn the consequences of her actions and maybe she'll make better decisions next time.

I cold heartily agreed with everything Robin said, I just hope she'll be okay. I told Robin that I'm supposed to go fishing with Shelvin and Myron but I can schedule it another time if she wanted me to. Robin told me she will be okay and to go ahead and have my fishing day out and she'll be just fine at the house. I told her okay and that we'll spend Sunday together. She agreed and told me she couldn't wait.

I texted both Myron and Shelvin and told them I could pick them up around ten this morning and we could pretty much spend the day catching fish and talking about our lives. I'm sure they have tons of questions about what went down with Airene and how she got caught up in something like that.

I guess I'll explain everything to them when we're all together. I went in the kitchen and fixed a loaf of bread for sandwiches, grabbed two big bag of chips, and a cooler of sodas and beers. We normally take turns to see who will get refreshments each time we go out fishing so it was my time to get everything. I grabbed my cell phone and my Off spray for those bats they call mosquitoes and headed out the door.

I'm really looking forward to this time away for a little bit to hang with the fellas, just to clear my head and escape away from the shit that went down with that trial yesterday. I wonder how Ryan is doing? I'll call him later tonight and see how he's holding up.

I blew the horn for Shelvin to bring his ass out of the house. He finally came out with his fishing rod. "Damn, what took your ass so long? I was just about to leave your ass," I said. "Man, your ass better not leave me," Shelvin said. I laughed as we gave each other dap when he got on the passenger side.

We went by Myron's house to get him. Myron was outside on the porch smoking a cigarette. "What's up man?" I said. "What's going on with you, Rob and Shelvin?" Myron said. "Trying to go catch these fish," I replied.

I pulled up to the lake and parked the car. We grabbed our food and the rest of our things, along with our lawn chairs. "Man, this is where it all began. We've been coming here ever since we all were about seven years old with our fathers. So almost forty-five years now," I said.

We put the bait on our fishing rods and threw it in the water. We sat waiting for the fish to start biting. "Man, so are you and Airene going ahead and getting a divorce?" Shelvin asked. "Yes, I think we are. There's no reason for us to stay married now, after what she's done to Ryan," I said.

Myron and Shelvin gave me an apologetic look. "Man, I'm really sorry this has happened to you and to Ryan. I guess you never really know a person and what all they're capable of. Whoever thought that little old woman, acting Airene would go through all that trouble just to try and set up Ryan? Do you think she was after Ryan for a while now, or do you think she just started this crazy revenge thing?" Shelvin asked. "I don't know man but I wouldn't put nothing past Airene's crazy ass. I guess she had more of an issue than I ever knew," I said. "You're right," Myron replied.

Myron looked like he was in deep thought. "Man, what's on your mind? You look like you're heavy in thoughts," I said. "I am. I met this young lady at the laundromat. Her name is Deloris. She's a nice looking lady, probably around forty-eight and she has four grown children. We've only been on two dates so far but it seems like things are going pretty good," Myron said. "Oh that's good," I said, trying to be encouraging.

Shelvin wasn't paying us any attention, like he was in a world all by himself. "What about you?" I asked. "What about me?" Shelvin finally chimed in to ask. "Have you met anyone yet?" I asked. "No, I haven't. No one wants me," Shelvin said laughing. "Ah man, there's always someone out there for everybody. Your problem is you like those damn Halle Berry type females," I said. "Man Rob what's wrong with wanting an attractive woman? I can't just wake up to anybody in the damn morning," Shelvin said, laughing. "I guess you're right on that. Just don't sit there waiting on someone like Halle Berry to come along that you miss out on someone nice," I said. "Yeah, you're right," Shelvin replied. "Well, life is too short to sit here settling for just anything to come your way. so if you're looking for something specific then maybe you'll find just what you're looking for if you be patient and wait on it," Myron said.

I was so relaxed out here fishing with my boys, as if I were in the comfort of my own home, watching the game and putting down a few beers. Just enjoying the peace and quiet. It was good to just hang out with the fellas today and relax for a change, without anyone calling and texting my phone, every twenty minutes or so. I texted my baby girl to see if she was okay. "Daddy, I'm okay but can Aijah come over for a while? Her mom and dad are going out for a while and she wanted to know if she could come over here?" Robin asked. "Yes, that's fine but no one else," I said. "Okay," Robin replied.

I'm thankful that I've never really had any problems with Robin or when Ryan was growing up. I'm thankful for that. Myron always stayed up at the school because either his son was fighting or cursing the teacher out, or just cutting school or something crazy.

Myron would often say he was sick and tired of running back and forth to the school, behind MJ not doing what he's supposed to be doing.

I used to sit back and listen when he would say that, wondering why he wasn't tightening up on MJ's ass for making him have to leave work and pick him up. I remember when Ryan left his report card home and I had to leave work early to pick it up and bring it to him and when he got home from school, I told him what would happen the next time I have to do that. Ryan made sure he never did that again.

We ate lunch and stayed about three more hours. It was such a nice and peaceful day, that no one wanted to leave.

CHAPTER 23

"Ryan"

Cornelius and I had our first date Friday night and I must admit, it was pretty cool and I really enjoyed myself. He told me he enjoyed our date as well. We enjoyed it so much that we planned another one tonight. I'm really looking forward to it. I think it's so much better since we already knew each other, compared to us meeting somewhere for the first time and deciding to go out.

I deleted my escorting website already the night that Dad and I went to the beach, when I got out of jail. That's a part of my life that I plan to leave in my past and never revisit. I've done a lot of things in my thirty years on earth that I'm not too particularly proud of. Dad told me I needed to stop what I was doing before I end up getting hurt or even killed.

I knew someone probably told him what I've been doing to make money. Dad never asked me about my clients or my personal life for that matter. He's never been the meddling type and I'm glad for that. I think if Dad knew just how much I was escorting, he would probably be shocked. I'm thinking he probably just thought I did it from time to time, just to earn extra money but I was doing it whenever time permits and I could get one person in and out, to get the next person in as well. He has no idea that it's been a source of income for me. This wasn't something I chose for myself. I had a lot of trauma and things that I dealt with as a child that my parents never knew about because I never told anyone. I guess I was afraid that some way they would blame me and say all this was my fault. Even the ones that made me out to be their prey that they taunted me each and every day and sometimes at night. One of these days, all of it is going to come out and my dad would know the kind of pain I carried with me from a child to an adult.

I took out my phone and mashed record so I could share it with my father, so if anything was to ever happen to me, he would see it and know what I went through. I finished the video and sent it to Jarod's email. I got up to see if Jarod was in his bedroom, which he was, reading a book, with the door halfway open. I knocked on his bedroom door. Jarod looked up and saw it was me and he told me to come on in.

I sat on Jarod's bed to talk to him. "What are you reading?" I asked. "The Unwanted Child," by John McCray," Jarod said. "Well is it good?" I asked. "It certainly is," Jarod said. "I couldn't help but stare at Jarod, because I know he knew exactly how that felt, to be "The Unwanted Child," which I'm sure a lot of people could relate to that title, even though I haven't read the book yet. "So what's up Ryan?" Jarod asked. "Look, I sent a video recording to your email. If anything was to ever happen to me, I want you to send it to my father but I don't want you to ever look at the video, unless something has happened to me, like I'm dead or something," I said.

Jarod looked at me like I was crazy or something. "You think someone is going to kill you or something?" Jarod asked. "I don't think so but hell you can never tell these days," I said. "Well that's true," Jarod replied. "I just want to be prepared if anything was to ever happen, that's all," I said. "Okay, I got you. So what are your plans tonight?" Jarod asked. "I have a date tonight," I said. "Oh nice," Jarod replied.

I saw the way that Jaron was looking at me, as if me having a date was downright impossible or something. "Why you looking at me like that?" I asked. "Because I've never known you to have a date set up, other than when we dated when we were in college," Jarod said. "That's probably true but I'm changing things up a bit," I said. "Oh okay, well that's probably a good thing. Everyone deserves some happiness." Jarod replied. "Thank you. Let me get back so I can get ready," I said.

I went back to my room and started cleaning up and then I got ready for my date. Cornelius and I have been texting pretty heavy lately and I'm enjoying getting to know him more each day. I told him I was on my way to get a haircut and he joked, saying I was getting all handsome for him. I told him I was definitely doing that. Cornelius laughed and said I didn't have to try hard to do that.

I was starting to get a warm feeling inside like I may have someone that I'm really feeling but I don't want to overthink this and things don't work out for us or at least for me. My barber didn't have many people so he was able to get me in and out in about an hour and a half, which wasn't bad at all.

After I left from getting my haircut, I went to the gym to get a little workout in and then headed back home. I had about two hours to kill before I had to get ready for my date. I laid across the bed and before I knew it, I was knocked out. I was sleeping so good that when my alarm went off, I didn't want to get up. I knew after getting in the shower the water would wake me up.

I grabbed my things and jumped in the shower. I dried myself off and brushed my teeth, and started ironing my clothes. I looked at myself in the mirror after I got dressed and I think I look pretty good with my brand new pair of Jordans that I just took out of the box today. I threw on my Jordan cap and was ready to get on the road to meet Cornelius. Cornelius and I said we were going to wear some jeans and sneakers today so it wouldn't be like we're under or overdressed, which I hate when that happens.

I grabbed my keys off my dresser and headed out the door. I didn't realize I left the house a little earlier than I had planned to but I just figured I would sit in the parking lot until Cornelius gets here.

The interstate wasn't bad, which was surprising for a Saturday night. I pulled up in the parking lot of the bowling alley and parked. I texted Cornelius and told him I was here at the bowling alley and that I got here a little earlier and I'll just be sitting here waiting until he gets here. He replied back saying "Okay." I was sitting in the car listening to Keyshia Cole, when my phone started to ring. It was my Dad calling.

I turned the radio down to answer my phone. "Hey Dad. What's up?" I said. "Hey son, I'm home with your sister and her best friend. What you up to?" Dad asked. "Oh, I'm in the bowling alley parking lot, waiting on Cornelius," I said. "Oh so you two are going bowling tonight huh?" Dad asked. "Yes we are," I said. "Well that's good. I'm glad to know you're hanging out with someone who's career oriented and has a good head on his shoulders. Well I'm not going to hold you up, so have a great time son and I love ya," Dad said. "Thanks Dad and I love you too," I replied, hanging up the phone.

Cornelius just texted that he was looking for a park. I waited for a few minutes and then I got out of the car when I saw him walking around to the front. I met him in the front of the building. "What's up mister?" I said, holding out my hand. Cornelius shook my hand, grabbing me into a bear hug. "It's good to see you Ryan," Cornelius said, holding open the door for me to walk in.

We checked in up front and I grabbed my credit card, prepared to pay my portion. "Don't worry about it Ryan, I got it this time," Cornelius said. "Are you sure?" I asked. "Yes I am. I can definitely afford to take you on a nice date," Cornelius said. "Okay, I accept that," I replied.

The young lady put us on lane twenty-two. Cornelius and I put on our bowling shoes and went around looking for a ball to fit our fingers. I put our names on the score machine and started our game. "Ryan are you a good bowler? I should've asked that before we decided to go bowling right?" Cornelius said.

I put Cornelius' name in first so he would be the first to bowl, just so I could see his bowling style. Cornelius got a six and then he picked up the spare on the next bowl. I got a strike, followed by another strike and two more strikes. "Man, I should've known your ass was setting me up," Cornelius said laughing. "I'm not setting you up. We're just having fun," I replied, laughing. I never told Cornelius that I was in the bowling league when I was in the ninth grade, up until I graduated from college.

Dad would take my mom and I every Sunday to bowl. It was good practice for me when I knew I was going up against my opponents that week. Cornelius and I played three games and I beat him in all three but not badly.

After we went bowling, we went out to dinner, which I was glad for because bowling will certainly make you build up an appetite. I was actually enjoying hanging out with Cornelius. He made me laugh the entire time. We sat across from each other and he looked at me and smiled. "I'm really glad we took the chance to get to know each other but I like the guy that I'm seeing. You're really easy to talk to and I like that," Cornelius said. "You are as well. At first when I asked you out the first time, I didn't know if we would hit it off but we did. I'm glad we're hanging out as well," I said.

After dinner we got a few drinks and continued talking and hanging out. I think Cornelius is like me and can't wait to see where this can actually go. Our date had finally come to an end and I suddenly became a little sad. I don't know why but it was like I wasn't going to see him again, which is crazy.

Cornelius dropped me back off to my car and we finally had our first kiss. It was exactly what I expected it to be and I must say I'm not disappointed at all. I just got back home. It was one-thirty in the morning.

I jumped in the shower and brushed my teeth. I lit some candles in my bedroom and played some music on my Bluetooth speaker. I dropped asleep before I knew it. I was knocked out, I guess the alcohol is what put me to sleep so fast. I jumped up when I heard someone knocking loudly on my front door.

I got up and went to the door. "Who is it?" I asked, opening the door. I don't know why I keep opening this damn door but I was just waking up not thinking rationally. The door swung open, almost hitting me in the face. "What the hell are you two doing here?" I asked. "You better stop raising your damn voice!" the man said. "This is my damn house and I'll raise my damn voice if I want to!" I yelled. "We'll see about that," the other guy said as he pulled out a gun and pointed it at me. "Get your ass in that damn room!" the man said, as he pushed me in front of him and pointed the gun in my back, forcing me inside my room.

The other man closed my door behind us and then walked up on me and put the gun to my forehead and pressed it hard. "What are they about to do to me?" I said, to myself. My damn gun is in the bottom of my nightstand and there's no way I can get to it with two of them in here like that. I could possibly fight off one but not two. These guys aren't small guys at all.

I jumped up off the bed and jumped in one of the men's face and he hauled off and punched me in my stomach as hard as he could, knocking the damn wind out of me. The other guy jumped on top of me and put his hands around my throat. I tried to fight him off but he kept squeezing harder and harder, trying to kill me. I couldn't breathe, as I was trying my best to fight to gasp for air.

I knew I couldn't fight both these men off and it seemed like everything was closing in on me, as I blanked out. I immediately felt something over my face and I tried fighting, to get some air but I couldn't. They were just too strong and I knew I was no match for them. I used every strength I had but I could no longer do it. "God, please forgive me for everything I've done and I'm asking you to watch over my dad and my little sister." I knew it was the end and I wasn't afraid to go but I didn't want to leave my family and Cornelius like this, without saying a proper goodbye, but some things were just out of our control and this was definitely one of those times.

CHAPTER 24
"Robert"

I got up and showered and then got Robin up for church. I went to the kitchen and made pancakes, eggs and bacon. Robin finally came to the table. "Good morning Daddy," Robin said. "Good morning baby girl. How did you sleep?" I asked. "I slept good. Now I'm ready for breakfast," Robin said, fixing her breakfast and sitting down at the table next to me.

I must admit that since Airene has been out of the house and locked up, everything has been so peaceful here and that's what I like. I don't have to worry about her bickering and aggravating me. Robin and I finished our breakfast and I did the dishes. "Dad, I'm going ahead and finishing getting ready for church," Robin said. "Sounds good baby girl," I said, drying the last plate.

I ran upstairs and started getting dressed for church myself. I sat on the bed and for some reason, I felt empty inside like I lost something that meant the world to me. I know I'm not feeling that over Airene, shit, we were barely even speaking before she left, so now that she's gone, I feel free and like a ton of bricks have lifted off my chest.

I grabbed my keys off the table, about to leave. "Robin, are you ready to go?" I asked. "Yes sir," Robin said, grabbing her purse as we walked out of the house, while I locked up the house. We got in the car and as I was backing up, a car pulled up behind my car, trapping me in my driveway.

I didn't recognize the car and I wondered why they just blocked me in my driveway like that. "Who is that Daddy?" Robin asked. "I don't know baby but they better get the hell out of our way so we can get to church," I said.

I waited for whoever was in the driver's seat to get out the car.

The young man got out of the car and walked towards us. "Baby, that's Jarod and Cornelius," I said, getting out of the car to see what Jarod and Cornelius wanted. "Good morning Mr. Jacobs," Jarod said, extending his hand towards me. "Hey Jarod, how are you?" I asked, shaking his hand. "Hey Mr. Jacobs," Cornelius said, extending his hand to me as well. "Hey Cornelius. Good to see you both, but I'm a little surprised to see you this morning, especially since we're on our way to church," I said.

Jarod dropped his head and started crying. "Mr. Jacobs, I came home this morning and I found Ryan in his bed unresponsive. I tried to feel for a pulse but Ryan was ice cold. Ryan was dead when I found him," Jarod said.

I felt my body go limp just before I was about to hit the pavement on my driveway. Jarod and Cornelius quickly grabbed me before I fell. "That can't be my son! My son can't be dead! Ryan can't be dead!" I kept saying it over and over in my head and out loud. Maybe the more I keep saying it, I'll wake up and someone can tell me that I was dreaming and it's not Ryan that was in his bed and he's alive. "Jarod, please tell me you made a mistake and you thought Ryan was in his bed dead but it really wasn't him," I said.

Jarod shook his head and started crying again. "Jarod, tell me he was only resting," I said. I knew I had to sit down. Jarod and Cornelius helped me onto the porch as well. Robin must have been listening to her music in the car until she saw what was going on and she got out and started walking towards the porch. "Dad, what's wrong? Is everything okay?" Robin asked. "No baby, Jarod and Cornelius said that they found Ryan dead in his bed this morning," I said. "Oh my God!" Robin screamed, putting her hand over her mouth and crying.

I held my daughter in my arms as we both mourned the death of her brother and my son. Lord, they say life can sometimes throw a hard blow from time to time but this one really knocked me off my feet. "Jarod, does it look like he just died or does it look like foul play was involved and someone actually did something to him," I asked. "Mr. Jacobs, it looked like he just went to sleep but didn't wake back up. There's no signs that someone was ever in the house with him." Jarod said.

Cornelius got up from the porch and walked toward his car. He was shaking his head and he started hard down crying as he laid his head on top of the hood. Cornelius and Ryan just started spending time together and I could tell they were really liking each other. I can imagine how he must feel, thinking you finally found someone that you think you can establish something meaningful with, only to lose them to death.

I know Cornelius is wondering why God gave him that little hope and happiness, only to turn around and snatch it away from him, especially after he thought he had found the one that he had a chance with. There was something in Ryan's voice that made him smile whenever Cornelius' name was even mentioned. It's been a long time since I've seen him like that.

Jarod went behind Cornelius as Cornelius still had his head pressed on the hood of his car. Jarod hugged him and Cornelius really cried then. His tears and loud sobs pierced my heart for what he was going through.

Cornelius and Jarod finally walked back over to the porch. Robin seemed a little calmer and was now just staring at the tree in our front yard. "Dad, you remember when you had a little swing on that big branch out there and Ryan would come over and pushed me for hours on it. I would keep yelling, push me higher big brother, push me higher, and Ryan would tell me "Robin hood, if I push you too much higher, you could fall out the swing and it would be all my fault and I can't let nothing happen to my little sister.

Ryan would do anything he could for me. Now my mother and my brother are gone. Daddy, everyone is leaving us. All we have is each other now," Robin said. "That's true baby, everyone is just leaving us. We're both going to get through this," I said. "We sure will," Robin said.

"Mr. Jacobs, if you don't mind may I stay here for a few days? They are doing their investigation on the townhouse since it's now a crime scene?" Jarod said. "Of course you may stay with us for as long as you like," I said. "Thank you Mr. Jacobs. Look, the coroner said he would need you to come down to the morgue to identify

Ryan's body. I told him we could do it, just to spare you the pain of having to do that but he said he would need the consent from a parent if he had a parent still alive and was in their right state of mind.

But if you're not up for doing that today, I'm sure you can go tomorrow or the day after. Today is already a hard day for you," Jarod said. "Yes it is Jarod, but I think I need to do this today, just to go ahead and get it over with," I said. "I understand that. If you want us to go with you, we can do that now," Jarod said. "It's up to you but I would like you both to go with us," I said. "Okay we can do that," Cornelius said.

I grabbed my keys out of the car and locked the car. Cornelius said we could all ride with him over there to the morgue and he would bring us back home after we're done.

It seemed like we got here so fast. We got out of Cornelius' Mercedes and walked inside the building. I told the lady up front that we were here to identify my son's body, "Ryan Jacobs." The receptionist told me that someone would be here shortly to help me.

We waited for about ten minutes, when a dark-skinned, heavy set man came through the double doors. "Mr. Jacobs, I'm Mr. Lewis, the coroner here. We need you to identify the body so we can go ahead and start working on the body as soon as possible," Mr. Lewis said. "Okay, I understand," I said. "Well if you're all family then you all can come on back with me now," Mr. Lewis said. We all followed Mr. Lewis as he went through the double glass doors.

We stood in a hallway for a few minutes as Mr. Lewis told me he had to pull the body out. We just stood there looking around and waiting until Mr. Lewis comes back. "Lord, I never thought I would have to identify one of my children at the morgue or have to bury them. I always prayed that one day my children would have to bury me and not the other way around. This has to be one of the hardest things I ever had to do in my life," I said. "I can only imagine Mr. Jacobs but at least you don't have to do it by yourself. We're all here together," Jarod said. "Thanks," I replied.

Mr. Lewis brought the body out in a room. He then waved for us all to come inside. We gathered around the body, waiting for Mr. Lewis to remove the sheet that was over the body on the table and I prayed like I never prayed before that this person wasn't my son. "God please don't let this be my son. Lord let this be a mistake. Let this be a mistake and it's not Ryan," as I prayed out loud. Mr. Lewis removed the sheet. It was definitely Ryan's body. My tears had returned as I touched my handsome son's face, wondering what happened to him. "Lord, who would do this to you Ryan? Who would take your life like this?" I said. "I'm sure we'll find out the truth, once and for all," Jarod said. "Yes we will," I replied.

I nodded my head for Mr. Lewis to take Ryan's body away. "Mr. Lewis, I want a full autopsy on my son. I want to know how he died," I said. "Okay Mr. Jacobs, I'll get on that as soon as possible. You all may head out through the same door you came through to this room and I'm so sorry for your loss," Mr. Lewis said, as he covered Ryan's body back up with the sheet. "Thank you," I replied, as we headed to the parking lot to get in Cornelius' car.

CHAPTER 25
"A Memory of Ryan"

I sat in my bedroom as people came to visit from the church and my job. A few of Ryan's coworkers, students and fraternity brothers came to show their respect. I couldn't stand to be around all these people but I allowed family and friends to be held at my house since Ryan wasn't married or had his own family.

The police haven't found any leads or anything. The autopsy was done and Mr. Lewis confirmed that Ryan was strangled and then suffocated to death. Whoever did this probably used their bare hands to choke Ryan and then probably grabbed a pillow to put over Ryan's face. I sure hope my son's murderer or murderers are punished for what they did to my son because Ryan was a good guy and a great son. He never tried to hurt or mistreat anyone. Ryan might have lived a promiscuous life but he was trying to leave that alone since he found someone that he truly liked and wanted to be with.

I wonder if he's at peace and if he made it into heaven? I tried not to think of that because no one knows the relationship that Ryan and God had and whether or not he repented for his sins and mistakes that he's made in his life, right before he died. I know that God is a forgiving God and he will forgive you for anything. Knowing that gave me peace for wherever Ryan is. I went back in the living room, to at least mingle with my guests. I didn't want to appear rude or anything but I'm sure people didn't really expect me to be all happy go lucky at a time like this. There's about thirty people in the house and maybe about twenty people outside.

A few people from the church made a meal and brought over. I definitely appreciated it but my mother always said, "you can't eat everything from everyone." Shannon wanted to come by but I told her, I don't think that would be appropriate to come to my house, especially since I'm still technically married and my daughter is here as well. Shannon acted like she couldn't understand but I wasn't in the mood to try to make her understand anything. I'm only concerned about my baby girl right now.

Robin had her moments that she would break down and other moments she would isolate herself from everything and everyone, which I can't say that I blamed her.

Myron and Shelvin have been my rock through it all. They were like Ryan's uncles and were there if Ryan ever needed them. They made sure I'm good, in case I needed anything.

Alexandria's parents and her siblings came over to show their respects and to offer their condolences. They pretty much abandoned me and Ryan when I married Airene. I guess they felt like there was no room for them, which I never felt that way. Jarod had been staying here since they were still investigating the townhouse. I told him he could stay here as long as he wanted to. Ryan always told me that Jarod never knew who his father was because he abandoned his wife and Jarod when she was pregnant with him. I guess that's why Jarod always looked up to me as a father figure, which I never minded.

It's important to have both Jarod and Cornelius around since they both were important to Ryan. Ryan's two best friends, Anita and her twin brother Aneil both came over and brought some food. Anita and Aneil were our next door neighbors when they were kids. Anita and Aneil went to live with their grandmother after their father shot their mother to death, when they were sixteen. The father was sentenced to life in prison.

That broke Ryan's heart when they had to move away. Ryan felt abandoned and that he was losing everyone that was in his life. Ryan stayed in touch with both of them after they got out of high school and went off to college. Jarod asked me if there was anything that I wanted of Ryan's from the townhouse and I was welcome to come get them. I thanked him and told him that after all this is over with, Robin and I will definitely come by.

The school board came by and offered their condolences about Ryan's death and they told me that they were going to administer a check to Ryan for all he had to go through at the school with the investigation and to find out that Ms. Smith was behind it. So they handed me a check for fifty-thousand dollars and they gave me all the money that was in Ryan's 401K which was about fifty-thousand dollars as well. They told me hopefully the money will take care of the funeral expenses as well as some other bills as well. I thanked them and told them to stay for a while. They stayed for about an hour which was longer than I expected them to.

I looked over at Jarod and he looked so lost, like he doesn't know what he's going to do next. Ryan had told me that Jarod has been late on their rent on many different occasions so he didn't know how long he was going to let him continue to stay there with being late all the time. I know Jarod wouldn't want to live with us forever but I want to know that he'll be okay and I'm not going to leave him high and dry. Jarod has no idea that Ryan's house is already paid for. Ryan told me that if anything was to happen to him to leave the townhouse to Robin when she is grown but until then the house would be willed to me. I think I'm going to let Jarod live there and I'm going to make sure he'll be alright when all this is over with.

I saw Myron and Shelvin over there talking to him and Cornelius, as well as Alexandria's brothers and sisters. They both seemed like they were okay. Alexandria's family didn't say a word to Robin and I was ready to throw their asses out but Robin told me it was okay and for me to try to keep the peace at least until all this is over with. I told her I would definitely try.

Robin laughed because she knows how I get when it comes to the happiness of my children. I went to the kitchen to make sure Jarod and Cornelius were both okay. They told me they were but Cornelius told me he was going to go sit on the back porch for a while just to be by himself for a moment. I nodded my head because he looked like he needed that. I hope that Jarod and Cornelius can help each other through this. They're both nice, well-mannered guys. There's no telling, maybe Ryan's death will make them lean on each other as more than friends.

I grabbed two beers out of the fridge and went and checked on Robin. A few of Robin's friends were up in her bedroom with her.

I knocked on the door and walked in. They were all just playing Uno on Robin's bed. "You okay sweetheart?" I asked. "I'm okay Daddy. My friends are keeping me company," Robin said. "Okay good. Well if you all get hungry, there's plenty of food in the kitchen," I said. "Thanks Dad. Thank you Mr. Jacobs," Robin and her friends said, as I closed her bedroom door and went into the living room.

I needed a moment to myself and to get away from everyone. I decided to join Cornelius on the back porch. Cornelius looked up at me and tried to smile but he burst out crying. I walked up to him and gave him a fatherly hug. Cornelius seemed like he just needed a hug because he really let go and broke down. "Get it out son. There's no one out here but you and me," I said.

Cornelius finally lifted his head up and I handed him one of the beers. "Cornelius, no one expects you to not miss Ryan. I know how close you two were becoming and I was glad to know that he had someone like you in his life," I said. "It's so unfair Mr. Jacobs. I finally found someone I wanted to spend my life with and after two dates, two freaking dates, he's gone and never coming back." Cornelius replied. "I know Cornelius. I know it seems so unfair but that's how I felt when my Alexandria died, Ryan's mother.

Ryan was so close to his mother. He was so close to her that I would get jealous because I wanted that closeness with my son like he had with his mother. Ryan knew how much I loved his mother and I knew how much he loved her, so what we did instead of pulling away and resenting one another, we pulled together and that's how we became so close. That's why we're as close as we were before he died. We spent so many years when he was younger disconnected from each other.

Cornelius, I'm so thankful that Ryan and I did everything in our power to become close because if we didn't, his death would've probably made me lose it. I can only think about our happy times and moments together, because that's what is going to get me through these hard and rough days. Our good, happy memories together.

I have the memories when he would try so hard to make the "A" honor roll because he wanted to prove it to himself and make me proud of him. I always told Ryan that I'll always be proud of him whether or not he got straight "A's" or not. I told him he couldn't just get anything on a test but as long as he did his best, I would always be proud of him. When Ryan was in the ninth grade he was determined he was going to get on the A honor roll. Ryan wouldn't go out to play with his friends or anything during the week. Ryan barely even turned the TV on in his room, all he did was study. He made studying his entire life.

Ryan would do questions in the chapters, write down all the definitions and all before they even got to the chapter. Ryan read the entire history book, as well as his science book before the semester was over. When Ryan got his first nine weeks report card and he had all "A's" except one B. That boy had a damn fit and nearly freaked out. Ryan went to the principal that next day and told him that his teacher made a mistake and didn't give him the right grade because he should've got an "A."

Ryan's principal didn't pay him any attention and told Ryan he should be proud of his grades and that a "B" wasn't the end of the world. After Ryan went to the principal three days in a row and the principal told Ryan the same thing, he told his principal that it was going to be his last time coming to him and that he was going to the school board.

Ryan said that's when the principal finally took him seriously and did some investigation of his own and he and Ryan went to his History teacher and took all his tests that he did in the class with him. The principal asked for all of Ryan's test scores and grades and he averaged them up himself.

Ryan's grade came out to a ninety-two which was two points from being an "A." Ryan showed the principal as well as his teacher all of his test scores, which none of his test scores were below a ninety-two and he had mostly one-hundreds on all his test and quizzes. So when the principal looked at his scores, and compared it to Ryan's tests, he saw that he had a seventy-five. Ryan told his teacher he's never got a seventy-five in his life so when the teacher looked at his test that Ryan had, he realized that he must have mixed up his grade with someone else and on that particular test Ryan got a ninety-six, which brought his average to a ninety-seven. The principal and the teacher quickly apologized to Ryan and promise they would give him his recognition and give him all his awards and certificates he was supposed to get, plus make an announcement to correct it the next day.

Ryan was so happy that he stood up for himself and he said he knew he had worked his behind off that entire nine weeks and to not give him his "A" that he knew he earned and deserved was not going to fly with him.

When Ryan told me that story, I couldn't have been more proud of him because he knew his worth, he knew what he had earned and he knew what he deserved, so he wasn't going to settle for what the teacher gave him because he knew what he had done to get his "A."

Cornelius, that's probably why Ryan hasn't really dated and wanted to work towards a real relationship with anyone, until he met you, because he wasn't going to just settle for anything he knew what he had earned, what his worth was and what he knew he deserved.

I know it seems unfair that you feel that you were cheated out of or what could've been but God has someone else for you, just let what I shared with you about that story to allow you to wait for what you deserve, for you to know your worth and never to just settle for anything," I said.

Cornelius gave me a warm smile because deep down I think he knew exactly what I was talking about. I shared a lot more stories with Cornelius as we continued sitting on the back porch, as we shared memories of Ryan.

CHAPTER 26

"Sleep Well Ryan"

Cornelius and Jarod came over around ten o'clock this morning already dressed for the funeral. I asked them how their night was but all they did was just smile. I smiled as well because I could see that they were both getting closer each day that they were trying to be there for one another.

Robin came and sat in the living room with Jarod and Cornelius. I went upstairs to my room to get dressed and get myself together. I can't believe I'm preparing myself to go to my thirty-year old son's funeral today. Thirty years is nowhere near long enough for someone's life but it's not up to me to decide that. I just knew that Ryan accomplished a lot in his thirty years of living. Valedictorian, with a 4.5 GPA from high school. He earned his Master's degree and had his dream job as a seventh grade Science teacher.

Ryan was on the track team, and on the basketball team as a valuable player. Ryan was in the marching band, beta club, mock trial, drama club, debate team, and a major in the ROTC program. Ryan had a lot going for himself and someone took all that away from my son.

I looked in the mirror one last time before grabbing my phone and I think I'm ready to say goodbye to my son, for the last time. I grabbed my keys and headed back in the living room. People started coming by the house. Robin looked at me and smiled. "Daddy, I know you'll be glad when all this is over with?" Robin said. "Baby girl, you don't know the half of it," I said. "Trust me Daddy, I do. These dang people come over here and don't know when to take their behinds home, like we want to sit here and look up in their faces and half of them don't even bring anything like a jug of water or anything so that tells me, they only came to eat," Robin said.

Cornelius and Jarod both burst out laughing. "I swear you can tell you're Ryan's sister alright. You both don't care what you say," Jarod said laughing. "And believe me Rod, we get it from our dad," Robin said. "I'm not that bad," I replied. "Yes Daddy, you are," Robin said.

The funeral home finally came and they had us lined up for the ones that were riding in the family car. They asked me who all was riding in the family car. "You both are riding with us right, Jarod and Cornelius?" I asked. "Yes sir, if that's okay with you?" Cornelius said. "That's definitely fine with me," I said. "Dad, what about your formal mother-in-law and father-in-law? Do you think they would like to ride in the family car with us?" Robin asked. "Well Ryan wasn't close to them like that anyway. I guess they thought Ryan's lifestyle wasn't pleasing and accepting into their family, so when Alexandria died, they died right along with her in Ryan's life," I said. "So sad," Robin replied.

We all got in the car. I asked Anita and Aneil, Ryan's old friends that he grew up with to ride with us as well as Myron and Shelvin. They all agreed. We got to the church and lined up to go inside. I looked right into Shannon's face as I walked in with Robin. I quickly smiled and nodded my head to her. Jarod and Cornelius were behind us, followed by Anita, Aneil and Myron and Shelvin.

I told the funeral director that I wanted Ryan's casket opened during the first part of the service, that way everyone could view him as they come in and that would be it. I wanted him to have a celebration of his life and not people hard down screaming and have to be carried out of the church or any of that mess. Mrs. Davis told me she understood and that my wishes would be followed through.

I stood over Ryan's body, holding on to his hand, not wanting to let him go. "How do I say goodbye to my only son? How do I let him go for good? How do I cope without seeing him and hearing his silly laughter, when he said or saw something funny? I can't imagine not seeing Ryan's face again at the dinner table on Sundays. Lord give me strength to get through this. Give me strength to make it without my son. Ryan, I'm going to do everything in my power to try to find whomever is responsible for your death to get what they deserve." I leaned over and kissed Ryan on the forehead and on the side of his cheek for the last time. "Sleep well my prince, until we meet again," I whispered, as I lifted up my head and dried my tears.

Robin mourned the loss of her brother for the last time, as I held my arm around her. The ushers gave everyone an obituary in the church. The funeral was extremely packed but the church was big enough to accommodate everyone that was here without anyone standing up. The funeral director sent up three men to close the casket after everyone viewed Ryan's body. As they began to close the top of the casket, my heart felt like it was going to jump out of my chest. "God my only son! My only son is gone!" I yelled. Robin grabbed my hand and squeezed it. I knew this day wasn't going to be easy for me but I had no idea it was going to hit me like this. This is a pain that no father should have to go through. I prayed again to God to just give me strength to get through this.

The service started and the choir sang "I'm standing in the need of Prayer." Brother Raymond Johnston sung it and he sounded just like the artist. That's always been one of my favorite songs and Ryan loved it as well. Sister Regina Brown, sang "Thank you," by Bernita Washington. The service wasn't sad at all. Reverend Charles came with the scripture, that made the hair stand up on my arm. He read from Ecclesiastes 3:1-8, "For everything there is a season, and a time for every matter under heaven; a time to weep, and a time to mourn and a time to dance. Reverend Charles then went to Psalm 30:5, "weeping may endure for a night, but joy cometh in the morning. That's what God laid on my heart to preach about in this time of need. My message was in that very scripture, "I'm going to read it again, in case the ones in the back that were too busy looking around at who's crying and what they have on, how pretty their shoes are, then to be paying attention to what I said. "I said, Psalm 30:5, weeping may endure for a night, but joy cometh in the morning. So my sermon is "But Joy," Pastor Charles said.

Pastor Charles didn't come to play around today, with his

sermon, he told us that he didn't come to preach to the dead, he came to preach to the living, and that's exactly what he did. If I could see Ryan's face right now, he would be waving his hand and saying, "Preach it Pastor." After the service was over, we did the burial in the church cemetery, beside Alexandria. When my time comes, I want to be buried beside my first love Alexandria, and my son as well.

We all went to the fellowship hall and ate together. I wanted to leave the funeral and come home to relax and not invite any of these people back to my house but I knew this was going to be the last day so I decided to hold it in for one more day and then we all could get back with our lives.

Everyone finally left the house which was nine-thirty. That was one of the best feelings to see all these people leaving. I told Robin during the summer she and I are going on vacation and she could pick anywhere she wanted to go. We both needed a vacation to relax our mind because this was more than I could handle.

Now everyone was going back to their normal lives and Ryan may or may not be remembered but he will definitely be remembered by us, the people that truly loved him. I went to my bedroom to get out of this suit and to take a hot shower. I wanted to have a glass of wine and listen to some music and just relax and reflect on the wonderful memories I have of my son.

I gathered my things to take my shower when the house phone rang. I picked up the phone, "Hello," I said. "You have a collect phone call from the womens institution in Gastonia NC. Will you accept the charges?" the recording asked.

I wanted to hang the phone up and say, "hell no," but I went ahead and accepted it. "Hello," I said. "Hey Robert," Airene said. "Hello," I replied. "How are you doing?" Airene asked. "I've been better but I'll make it," I said. "I heard about Ryan and I want to say I'm sorry for your loss," Airene said. "Thank you," I replied. "Look at it this way, at least he didn't die of Aids," Airene said. It took everything in me to not curse this trick out from everything under the damn sun but I refused to give her dumb ass any of my anger that I had built up inside of me. Airene's ass wasn't even worth my damn time. "Hold on," I said.

I went to Robin's bedroom and knocked on her door. "Come in," Robin said. "Hey baby girl, look your mother is on the phone, would you like to talk to her?" I asked. "No! I have nothing to say to her and please tell her to not call here again, unless you want to talk to her, otherwise I'm done," Robin said.

I didn't want to be the one to tell Robin to talk or not talk to her, I wanted that to be her decision to make. "Baby, are you sure?" I asked. "Yes Daddy. My mother became dead to me when she tried to send Ryan to jail and get him fired from his job. Anyone that would do something like that to another human being, especially their stepson, is not a person I want to be associated with. So Daddy please tell her to never call here again," Robin said. "Okay sweetheart, I will," I said, closing her bedroom door.

I went back to the phone. "Hello Airene, look Robin doesn't want to talk to you. She said to tell you not to ever call this house again and I feel the same way," I said, hanging up the phone. I was about to block the number but I decided not to. I was done with Airene all together and from the looks of it, so was Robin. The last thing I have to get her to do is to sign the divorce papers so I can be done with her for good.

CHAPTER 27

"Back to Reality"

I went back to work today. It actually felt good getting out of the house and getting back in the swing of things. Everyone at work welcomed me back with open arms and I thanked everyone for their calls, texts and visits. I told everyone that their acts of kindness definitely didn't go unnoticed.

Shannon was there to welcome me back with open arms and to be honest, I was glad to see her. It felt good to see her beautiful face and nice curvy body. Shannon talked about us moving on with our lives with each other. I told her I wasn't ready for a committed relationship and plus I'm still married. I told her I can't start a new book in my life right now, until I'm sure I'm done with the old one, which I know for sure I am.

Shannon acted like she understood but deep down I don't know if she did or not. I had to reschedule my inspections from last week to this week since I was out all of last week. Mr. Johnson knocked on my office door. "Come in," I said. "Hey Robert. I just wanted to offer my condolences for the passing of your son. I lost my son David in a car accident three years ago and when I tell you I think I cry every day since he passed away. This feeling will never go away but each day you'll find it gets a little easier to move on. You grieve as long as you need to and don't let anyone tell you, you should be over with that process by now. People will say anything when they're not the ones dealing with it.

So please let me know if you need anything or you need to take a few more days off or something. I will continue to keep you and your family in my prayers," Mr. Johnson, said. "Thank you Mr. Johnson, I really appreciate it," I said. "You're more than welcome. Have a blessed day Robert," Mr. Johnson said, before leaving my office.

I think I might have come back to work a little too soon. I feel like I haven't really grieved like I'm supposed to. "Ryan, Lord knows I miss you so much. I know you're in a better place but I just want to see your face, your handsome smile and your cheerful voice, that you love to change it up to imitate someone just to make me laugh. I need to press on Ryan, because if love could've kept you here longer with me, you would still be here with us.

The police said they're still looking for your killer but I don't know if they really are or they're just telling me that just to make me think that they haven't given up but deep down they have. All I know is there's still no leads and no arrest has been made. I have faith that your murder won't go unsolved. I believe there's an answer and it will be revealed one day."

I glanced at the clock and saw that it was twelve o'clock. I promised myself that I would go by Ryan's and Jarod's place and see if I would like to take any of Ryan's things as a keepsake. I think I'll do that after I leave work today. I'll pick Robin up from school and we'll go straight over there. I took out my phone and texted Jarod and asked him if five-thirty will be good to come get some of Ryan's things today. Jarod said that would be fine.

I grabbed my keys to go to lunch, not having an idea of what I wanted to eat. I didn't bring anything to eat but I'm sure, I'll find something just by riding around. I saw "Smoke Pit" over by Target and decided on a barbeque sandwich, which would probably fill me up.

I sat down by the window in the restaurant and ate my lunch. I was in deep thought, when I saw this young white couple that walked in and took a seat. I noticed they had two children that looked about six and nine years old. The little boy was the oldest I assumed since he was so much taller than the little girl.

Everyone was looking at the young family because the little boy was dressed like a girl and the little girl was dressed like a little boy. That's one thing I would never condone. If your child is gay that doesn't mean you did anything wrong as a parent, but to be buying them clothes like that is a little too much. If they don't have jobs, then the way they dress is still your responsibility as a parent to buy them clothes for the gender that they are. I would've never bought Ryan a damn dress to put on as a child and buy Robin big baggy pants and tee-shirts that are two sizes too big for her to wear. I feel as a parent, you have a right to tell your child what to wear and what not to wear, because as long as they're a child, you can control what goes on in your house.

I just finished my lunch when the little boy turned around and saw me and he waved. I waved back at the young man and then he turned and said something to his father and they both got up and walked toward me. "Hello Mr. Jacobs, my name is Caden Bryant. Your son Mr. Jacobs was my Science teacher, and he was the best teacher I ever had. I'm so sorry for your loss and I'm praying for you and your family as you're going through your loss," Caden said. "Thank you so much Caden, that was really nice for you to say that. We're dealing with my son's death one day at a time. It's not easy but I believe God will give us the strength to go through this," I said. "I'm sure he will Mr. Jacobs. I'm Michael Bryant, Caden's father and when he saw you he said "Dad, that's Mr. Jacobs father, can I say hello to him," I told him he could but I was going to walk over with him. Mr. Jacobs we're not going to hold you up but we hope they find Mr. Jacobs killer or killers and justice will be served." Mr. Bryant said. "Thank you and I sure hope so as well," I said, shaking Mr. Bryant's hand and Caden's hand as well before leaving.

I grabbed my keys and headed out the door. I know they didn't mean any harm but the constant reminders make it a little hard to try to move on but I know it will eventually get better after a while. I pulled up in the parking lot and walked back to my office.

Shannon was sitting at her desk. "Hello, how was your lunch Shannon?" I asked. "It was good, I just grabbed some chicken fingers from KFC," Shannon replied. "Oh okay. I had a barbeque sandwich from Smoke Pit and some tea," I said. "Oh okay. Nice," Shannon said.

Shannon looked like she didn't have much to say to me. Maybe she thinks I'm playing games with her, which isn't the case at all. I think she just wants more than I'm willing to give her right now.

I won't be rushed into anything and that includes being with her. I finished everything up today in a timely manner. Not a bad day for my first day back in a week.

I guess I'll go pick Robin up now and head over to Jarod's place. I texted Robin before I left the office and told her I was on my way so be ready when I get there. She said she would be at our designated spot.

I got to the school at five-fifteen to pick Robin up. "Hey Daddy. How are you and how was your first day back to work?" Robin asked. "Hey sweetheart. It was okay but a little challenging," I said. "Why challenging?" Robin asked. "Because it seems like everyone kept giving me their condolences for Ryan, which I appreciated but sometimes it's just hard to move on if you're constantly hearing that over and over," I said.

"Dad you're so right. I must have heard I'm sorry for your loss about thirty times today as well," Robin said. "It will get better baby, I promise," I replied. "Okay, because I sure can't wait for it to get better," Robin said.

I just smiled at Robin's comment as I parked the car. I grabbed a box of garbage bags to put whatever I wanted to take with me. I texted Jarod and told him I was outside, about to walk to the door in a few minutes. I just sat in the car looking straight ahead and not moving. Robin looked at me. "Dad, we're going to do this together and get through this together," Robin said. "I know sweetheart. This is the first time I'll be in Ryan's townhouse since his murder," I said. "I know Dad. It will be the first for both of us but like I said, we'll get through this together," Robin said. "Thank you baby," I replied, giving Robin a hug.

CHAPTER 28

"Still Holding On"

Robin and I walked to the front door and knocked. Jarod came to open the door. "Hey Mr. Jacobs and Robin," Jarod said, inviting us inside as he gave us both a hug. "How are you both doing?" Jarod asked. "I'm trying son. I really am," I said, noticing how bloodshot red Jarod's eyes were. I could tell he was still taking it hard and probably crying every day, which broke my heart. "I know the feeling," Jarod replied.

We sat down in the living room. "Mr. Jacobs, it feels like Ryan is still here. It's like he never left. I was in here watching TV and the water faucet came on like three times last night and the light started flickering on and off, as well," Jarod said.

"What! Jarod what did you do?" I asked. "I had to get real with Ryan, like he always kept it with me and I said Ryan, don't you start that shit tonight man. You know how scary I am and I'm not up for this shit tonight out of you," Jarod said.

Robin and I both burst out laughing. "I know that's right," I said. "Mr. Jacobs, you remember where Ryan's room is so help yourself," Jarod said. Robin and I went in Ryan's room. "Jarod, come here please? I asked. "Yes sir, Jarod said. "Ryan doesn't have any embarrassing things in here that Robin shouldn't see does he?" I asked. "Mr. Jacobs, I already removed them for you, so I think I have everything out the way," Jarod said. "Good and thank you," I replied. "Hell, I said embarrassing things that Robin shouldn't see but knowing Ryan, he probably has things my ass doesn't need to see either," I said to myself.

I opened Ryan's closet and saw two of his leather jackets hanging up. Robin is a little bigger than Ryan but he always wears his jacket a little bigger so it should fit Robin perfectly. "Sweetheart try this jacket on," I said. Robin tried the jacket and it fit and looked nice on her. "It fits Daddy," Robin said. It does and it looks nice on you. Do you want it?" I asked. "Yes sir, I do," Robin said. "Well it's yours," I said. I tried on the other jacket and It fit good on me as well. Ryan also had a letterman's jacket from the fraternity he pledged hanging up as well. I asked Robin if she wanted that jacket and she shook her head no. I decided to take that jacket with me, even though I knew it was way too small for me but I wanted something just to hang up of Ryan's in his old room.

Ryan had about six pairs of Jordans that I grabbed and put in two trash bags. Ryan's suits were too small for me so I knew I couldn't fit in any of those, as well as any of his jeans and pants. I did take a few of his baseball and basketball hats as well and all his trophies he had and his certificates, awards, diploma and his degrees. Ryan also had a nice TV in his room; I left that but I took his Bluetooth speaker and all of his R&B CD's as well as his rap music.

I looked in Ryan's drawers and saw a lot of pictures that he had of him and Jarod, pictures of his mom, pictures of me and him and pictures of him and Robin together. Robin and I will go through all his pictures later on and decide which ones she wanted.

Robin and I took everything to the car and put them in the trunk and some in the backseat. "Robin, is that all you want of Ryan's?" I asked. "Yes that's all I want," Robin said. "Okay, well do you want to tell Jarod bye?" I asked. "No, I can't go back in there Dad," Robin said. "Okay, understand," I replied.

I walked back inside to tell Jarod I was leaving. Jarod was sitting on the couch, watching TV. "Hey Jarod, I'm leaving," I said. "Okay, Dad," Jarod said. "Mr. Jacobs, I'm so sorry that I called you that. It just came out. I feel like I've been a part of your family for so long that you're like my dad as well, but I'm sorry, I wasn't thinking." Jarod said, as if he was embarrassed. "Don't worry about it son. It would be an honor for you to call me "Dad" if you wanted to," I said. "I would like that Dad," Jarod said. "Come over here and give me a hug son," I said. Jarod stood up and gave me a hug. "I could tell this meant a lot to Jarod and it meant a lot to me too. "I love you Dad," Jarod said. "I love you too son. I think Ryan would be happy to see us bonding the way we are," I said. "I think he would as well," Jarod said.

"Dad look, I know you have Robin with you but I need you to come back over here, as soon as you drop her off. There's something major that we need to discuss, that will crack Ryan's case wide open. I didn't want Robin to hear us talking so please come back as soon as you drop hcr off," Jarod said. "Oh my God Jarod are you serious? Why didn't you tell me about this sooner?" I asked.

"Trust me Dad, you needed to grieve like how a father should grieve for his son and be mentally prepared for the funeral. Now that everything is over with, I can tell you and give you everything I have. I haven't shared this with a soul and not even the police know about this," Jarod said. "Damn son, you're scaring me with this," I said. "I know but I'll explain it the best way I can when you come back," Jarod said. "Okay, I'll be right back," I said. "I'll be right here," Jarod said. "Okay. Give me between thirty and forty minutes," I said. "Okay," Jarod replied.

I walked back downstairs and got in the car. "You ready sweetheart?" I asked. "I sure am," Robin said. "Okay, look call Pizza Hut and get a delivery to the house. I have to take care of something but I'll be back shortly," I said. "Okay Dad," Robin said.

I dropped Robin at the house and we brought everything from the trunk and backseat inside. I reached in my pocket and gave Robin twenty dollars for her pizza. "I'll be back soon," I said. "Okay Dad. Drive safely," Robin replied. "I will," I said, getting in the car. Jarod said he has a lot to tell me and information that will crack Ryan's case wide open. I wonder what he knows.

CHAPTER 29
"The Ugly Truth"

I just pulled up and parked in the driveway of Jarod's townhouse. I got out and knocked on the door. Jarod came to the door. "Dad, come on in," Jarod said. "Look Jarod, before you tell me what you want to tell me, let me see something first," I said. "Okay," Jarod said, as he walked in Ryan's room with me.

I took off my shoes and climbed on the top of Ryan's bed. I lifted a piece from his ceiling and felt around up there. "Dad, what are you looking for?" Jarod asked. "When Ryan was a little boy, he would hide things in the ceiling all the time. I bet he has something up here," I said, feeling around. I felt a box up and I quickly pulled it down and placed it on top of the bed. "What is that?" Jarod asked. "It's a safe box but it's probably where Ryan kept his money," I said. The safe box had a six number passcode combination to it, in order for it to open.

I put in Ryan's birthday but it didn't open. I put in Robin's birthday month, the day and the year and it still didn't open. Maybe it's my birthday but it didn't open either. I knew what it was then, its Alexandria's birthday month, date, and year. I put Alexandria's birthday information in and the box opened right up. I opened the box and it was full of money. Just by looking at it, there had to be over twenty-five thousand dollars in here and maybe even more. "Look at all this damn money," Jarod said. "Right, help me count it," I said.

Jarod and I counted the money and Ryan had fifty thousand dollars in his safe box. "That's a lot of money," Jarod said. "Yes it is," I replied, closing the box up and handing it to Jarod. "Jarod it's all yours," I said. "Dad, I can't accept this kind of money. You could put it in a trust fund or college fund for Robin. I'm sure she could use that money for school," Jarod said.

"Jarod, yes Robin could definitely use that money for school when she goes off to college but Ryan has told me how you sometimes struggled to pay your bill on time, so this is a little nest egg for you to make sure you're able to pay them on time. You were paying Ryan rent to stay in this townhouse but Ryan was paying mortgage on it. Ryan had his life insurance set up that if something was to happen to him his townhouse would be paid for and he left it in my name. So this is what I'm going to do. Since I have a house and Robin is too young for a townhouse, you can stay here at least until Robin gets out of college and we'll decide what we're going to do then. So you have about eight years to save up your money so when that time does come, you'll be financially set to do what you need to do.

I'm also going to write you a check for fifty thousand dollars and you just deposit it in your checking account. Look Jarod, don't take this money in this box to the bank, because it will go as a red flag to the IRS and they'll be trying to audit you. So put this box in a safe place and you could set a combination that you know and can remember. Do you understand?" I said. "Yes sir I do," Jarod replied. "Good. I'll keep Ryan's car as a second vehicle in case I have to get work done on my vehicle or something," I replied.

I took out my checkbook and wrote Jarod out a check for fifty thousand dollars. "Jarod, this should hold you for a long time, especially with you not having to pay rent. All you have is lights, water, cable/ internet and your food. You should be able to pay all your bills in a timely manner now, especially since it's just you living here, so your light bill and water bill should come down tremendously and I'm sure you probably don't go grocery shopping like that so your monthly bills should be no more than four or five hundred dollars a month, so you definitely should be good now," I said. "Yes sir, I definitely will be," Jarod said. "Well good," I replied.

Jarod and I walked in the living room so we could talk. "Now tell me what's so important that you wanted to talk to me about and that you said could crack Ryan's case wide open?" I asked. Jarod sat beside me on the couch. "Dad, I know you don't know this but Ryan was an escort. He was sleeping with a lot of men and they would pay him for whatever he was doing with them. I guess that's where all that money came from we found." Jarod said. I just listened to Jarod because I already knew about his little website and what he did, but I played it off to Jarod. I didn't want him to think that I was condoning what Ryan was doing. "Dad did you know that?" Jarod asked. "No Jarod I didn't. I knew Ryan was living a promiscuous lifestyle but I didn't know he was selling his body for money," I said. "Yes, he was. Now Dad, this next part is probably going to make you look at me a little sideways when I tell you this but now I'm glad I did, otherwise I wouldn't know the truth about who killed Ryan," Jarod said. "Okay," I said, looking at Jarod strange already.

Jarod stood up from the couch where we were sitting. "Dad, follow me if you will," Jarod said. I got up and followed Jarod into Ryan's bedroom. Jarod pulled down something that was on the top of Ryan's dresser and another item that was on his bed, headboard and he handed it to me. "Jarod, what is this?" I asked. "Dad, it's two spy cameras that record everything. I put them up afraid that something could happen to Ryan, and I had my own personal reasons too," Jarod said, which I know exactly what that was about, with his nasty ass. "Dad, the cameras recorded Ryan's killers that night and there were two guys." Jarod said. "Two guys?" I said. "Yes, there was two guys," Jarod repeated.

Jarod went and grabbed some kind of box machine and hooked it up to the TV and he put in a tape. I watched the tape and it showed exactly what the coroner said happed to Ryan. Someone choked him and the other person put a pillow over Ryan's face and smothered him to death. The cameras showed how Ryan was trying to get away and how he was fighting for his life but they overpowered him and took his life.

I dropped my head and wept as my son's lifeless body was left on his bed, while these two damn cowards just walked away and left him there. "My poor son. I wish I knew what Ryan was going through. Why didn't he come to me and tell me what was going on? I could've helped," I said. "Ryan didn't want you to think bad of him or find out what was really going on," Jarod said.

Jarod went to his room and returned with a laptop. He sat back beside me and he went to his email. Jarod opened up a file and clicked on it. It was a video of Ryan. Ryan was talking and he revealed a lot of things I didn't know that happened to him as a child growing up. I cried and cried like a little baby, when Ryan told me everything he went through. "Jarod, why didn't Ryan tell me any of this? Why did he keep all this to himself?" I asked Jarod, as if he had the answers to all my questions. "I don't know Dad. I really don't know. I think Ryan just didn't want to hurt you and he knew telling you this would've hurt you to the core and Ryan didn't want to cause you that pain," Jarod said. "I'm sure that's the reason but It was my job to protect my son. I should've been there. I should've been there," I said. "Dad, you didn't know. Ryan just didn't know how to tell you," Jarod said. "Yes that's true but now I know and I promise you these motherfuckers will not get away with this.

Jarod, the shit is about to hit the ceiling. There's nothing more painful for a parent than to lose their child and have to bury them, but now I have to take matters in my own hands and defend my son's honor. It's time for me to start plotting my payback and revenge.

There's no way in hell, I'm going to allow those bastards to think they're going to murder my son and get away with it, while they're roaming around here, thinking that no one will ever know what they've done. They're going to know exactly what hell and pain feels like when I send their asses there. There's nothing like a father's pain, who knows that someone hurt their child, but I promise you they will definitely know my pain and hurt when I'm done with them. So now I guess I'll have to take justice into my own hands and I'll be the law and sentence these bastards myself.

CHAPTER 30
"Preparing and Planning"

I asked Jarod to drive Ryan's car over to my house and I'll drop him back off. Jarod agreed and gave me the machine with all the videos so I could see who all Ryan was involved with. Hell it could be some of these political men that have wives and children and living that DL lifestyle.

I should expose each of these sick ass men for their part in what they did to my son, even though they all paid Ryan for his services, it was still horrible and some of these men have big positions in the church and political positions as well.

Jarod dropped Ryan's car off in my driveway and gave me the keys, while jumping on the passenger side. "Dad, what are you planning on doing with the evidence and the truth about who killed Ryan?" Jarod asked. "I'm going to take care of it and you don't breathe a word about this to anyone, because Jarod no one knows about that camera and videos besides you and me and trust me son, that's how we need to keep it. If anyone was to know that you had it recorded, they could come looking for you. So please keep your mouth shut and let me take care of this," I said. "Okay Dad," Jarod said.

I pulled up to Jarod's townhouse and dropped him off. "Dad, please be careful," Jarod said. "I will son," I replied. I don't know if Jarod's intentions of putting cameras up in Ryan's bedrooms, were as pure as he wanted me to believe but either way I'm glad he did, otherwise Ryan's death would still be unresolved. I now have all the proof that I need to do what I need to do.

I went to Walmart and got a disposable phone. I called Cornelius up and told him what all I found out and what my plans were. And that I was going to need him to get me an unregistered gun that can't be traceable back to me. Cornelius told me he didn't feel right about doing this but after I broke everything down to him he told me he understood and that he would probably do the same thing as well.

I told Cornelius that's the only way I can get revenge for Ryan was to carry this entire plan on out. I told him he is the only person that knows what I'm planning and if I was to hear it again, I would know he told it. Cornelius told me he would follow through with my plan and he wouldn't tell a soul about our conversation. Cornelius told me he would call my house phone and tell me it's done and that he put the gun in the mailbox. I told him thank you for everything.

I finally got home and warmed up my pizza in the microwave and sat at the dinner table to eat before I got in the shower and prepared myself for bed. I just finished my pizza and was sitting down at the table to digest my food. I washed my plate out and was heading upstairs when I heard the phone ring. "Damn, should I answer it or should I just let the answering machine get it?" I decided to go ahead and answer it, to stop the person from calling, suddenly forgetting that Cornelius was supposed to call me and let me know when it was done.

I picked up the phone in the kitchen. "Hello," I answered. "Hey Robert. I'm not going to take up much of your time but I just wanted to ask you for a favor," Airene said. "Okay, what is it?" I asked, wondering why I didn't hear the recording about the collect phone call like I did last time. I guess Airene has persuaded someone to let her use their cell phone. "I want to know if you'll speak on my behalf and maybe they'll give me a lesser sentence for what went down with Ryan?" Airene asked.

I took the phone away from my ear and just looked at it, as if Airene could see the expression on my face or something through the phone. "Let me get this shit straight, Airene; you want me to speak on your behalf for a lesser sentence after you almost got my son fired and him sent to jail by filing false allegations on him, with a child, his mother, and the damn principal? You got some damn nerves. You wanted Ryan to go to prison for something that you caused. You set up all this shit and when it didn't turn out in your favor, you're asking me for fucking damn help? And you think I'm going to testify to the judge or jury so you get a little slap on the wrist?" I asked.

Airene didn't say anything, as if she was thinking how stupid that must have sounded to me. "Airene, you have lost that little bit of sense you have left in your damn head. If you think I'm going to do that shit. Don't you ever call here again. My lawyer will be contacting you with signing the divorce papers because I'm done with you. Our daughter doesn't want to have anything to do with you and I can't say that I blame her. You are a terrible person that don't think about anyone but yourself. Please lose this number and again, don't call here again," I said, hanging up the phone.

I blocked that number and the jail number as well. I refuse to let Airene upset me or Robin any more than what she's already done. I called up Myron and Shelvin afterwards. I needed to clear my head and just get away from everything. I wanted to tell them what I just found out about Ryan and what I was about to do. I know they'll probably talk me out of it but that's exactly what I need to hear. How in the world can I plan to do something like that, knowing I don't even like damn guns in the first place?

Myron told me that fishing with my boys was exactly what I needed to get my mind away from everything. I told him he was right so they both told me that six-o'clock would work for them. I hung up the phone and headed upstairs when the house phone rang again. I swear I have a hot phone tonight. "Hello," I answered. "Hey Mr. Jacobs it's in your mailbox," Cornelius said, hanging up the phone.

I almost forgot that Cornelius was supposed to drop off something in my mailbox. I went to the mailbox and saw something in a brown paper bag. It was a 9mm and a box of bullets. Damn Cornelius wasn't playing. I'm sure he knows a lot of damn thugs that he got off from prison, that hooked him up and owe him many favors. I wonder what else Cornelius could get his hands on.

CHAPTER 31

"A Father's Justice"

It seemed like it was time to get up when I basically just laid down, about four hours ago. I wish I could sleep for another two hours but I know I have to get up. Maybe a hot shower will wake me up this morning? I grabbed my things and jumped in the shower. I swear I went through a lot the past few months and it just seems like life wasn't letting up on me. I just hope my daughter and I can live a normal life and things will get back to normal.

I dried myself off and ironed my shirt and then got dressed. I went in the kitchen and put two pop tarts in the toaster, grabbed some water and then put two more pop tarts in the toaster for Robin. Robin came downstairs, looking all cheerful. "Good morning sweetheart," I said. "Good morning Dad. How are you?" Robin asked. "I'm okay but I could definitely use a few more hours of sleep," I said. "You and I both," Robin said, laughing. "Do you want a ride to school or you're going to ride with Stacey's mom?" I asked. "I'm going to ride with Stacey's mom," Robin said. "Okay baby. Well have a good day at school," I said. "I will Dad and you have a good day at work," Robin replied.

I walked out to the car and suddenly realized that I didn't hug and kiss my baby. I quickly turned around and went back inside the house. "Dad, did you forget something?" Robin asked. "Yes, I forgot to hug and kiss you and tell you I love you," I said. "Ah Daddy," Robin said, like she didn't want me to do that. "No ah Daddy. I lost one child already and if I had one more chance to hug Ryan and tell him how much I love him, that would be one of the best things in my life right now," I said, hugging and kissing Robin. "You're right Dad. You never know when you leave the house if that will be your last time seeing that person again, so I definitely feel you on that," Robin said.

135

I just walked in the building and spoke to everyone. Shannon was sitting at her desk, eating a banana. "Good morning Shannon. How are you?" I asked. "I'm fine Mr. Robert. I hope you are as well," Shannon said. "I am," I replied, heading to my office. I see Shannon is on this Mr. Robert type of shit again. I don't have the patience to even respond to that comment. I made sure I had everything in the system so I could head out shortly to do my inspections. I've been putting this off long enough but this morning, I'm going to get it done.

I had everything keyed in the computer. I told Shannon, I'll be back closer towards lunchtime. Shannon nodded her head, not even looking at me. I guess she is upset with me, since I'm not down for what she wants, which is why I didn't want to get involved with anyone at work in the first place.

I just finished up all my inspections and told them I would inform the insurance company of my results in about two weeks. I had about twenty minutes before lunchtime so I'll grab something while I'm out. I ordered two plates of spaghetti from Olive Garden and went and picked them both up. I decided to get one for Shannon as well. I didn't want her to think that I was dismissing her or anything like that. I just wanted her to know that I just had a lot going on and I was just trying to get things back situated in my life.

I picked up the food and brought it back to the job. "Shannon, did I have any phone calls or anything?" I asked. "No you didn't," Shannon said. "Good, look I brought you lunch," I said. "Oh that was nice of you. What did you get me?" Shannon asked, with excitement. "I got you spaghetti from Olive Garden," I said. "Oh thank you so much. I love Olive Garden's spaghetti," Shannon said, with a smile. "I'm glad to hear that," I said.

Shannon and I walked to the breakroom and ate our lunch. I explained everything to Shannon and told her I didn't mean to make her feel like I was ignoring her or didn't want her around because that definitely wasn't the case. I told her that I haven't thought about pursuing a relationship because I'm in the process of filing for a divorce and plus I'm still dealing with the loss of my son. She acted like she understood and told me not to worry about her.

I told Shannon I don't want her out of my life so if we could take things slow, one day at a time then maybe we could start seeing each other and not just sneaking around when it's convenient for us. Shannon smiled and told me she would like that. Shannon and I finished our lunch.

I was finally done with everything and was ready to hcad out. I looked at the clock and saw it was five-o'clock. I told Shannon that I was leaving and she was leaving as well. I walked her to her car and headed out to get Robin. "Hey sweetheart. How was school?" I asked. "It was okay Dad," Robin said, sounding sad. "What's wrong sweetheart?" I asked. "Oh I just miss Ryan. I miss my big brother, texting me in the morning saying "good morning big head" and he would text me at night and said, I hope you're done with your homework because you know you're going to be the first doctor in the family," Robin said. I know Robin and Ryan had always been close but I didn't know they texted everyday like that.

I saw the sadness in my baby's eyes and I wish I could take her pain away from her. Lord if missing Ryan could bring him back, he would be right here with us and right now. I suddenly felt my eyes get a little teary as I pulled up in our driveway. Robin grabbed her bookbag and walked inside the house.

I grabbed my fishing rod and all the stuff I normally take to the lake and put them in Ryan's car. I went upstairs and changed my clothes and put on something more comfortable, with some old sneakers. "Sweetheart, I'll be back shortly," I said. "Okay Dad," I'll see you later," Robin said.

I grabbed my keys and headed out the door. I picked Myron up first and he talked and had me laughing the entire time. I picked Shelvin up and he got inside and spoke to us but he was a little quiet. "You must have had a rough day or something?" I said. "Why you say that?" Shelvin asked. "Because you're really quiet," I said. "I know, just got a lot on my mind," Shelvin said. I didn't say anything else but that definitely didn't stopp Myron from running his trap.

We took all the equipment out of the car and put everything on the picnic table and sat down like we normally do. "You two have no idea how much I needed this," I said. "Trust me man, we know," Myron said. "You may know a little but you don't know the half of it," I said.

I got up from the picnic table and stood in front of Myron and Shelvin. "You two have been my best friends for forty-six years, since we were five years old, when we first went to kindergarten together. You two have been in both of my weddings and for the birth of my two children, as well as I was there for your children's birth as well. We've even been there for each other for the death of our parents and all. Most people would never know what we've been through together.

This lake is where we've spent a lot of our times together as boys, fishing with our parents, while we were running back and forth in the woods, doing what children do. So can you imagine the hurt and the pain I felt to know that you two have been molesting my son, since he was a little boy," I said.

Myron stood up when I said that. "Rob, what the hell are you talking about?" Myron asked. "Sit your bitch ass down!" I yelled pulling out my gun from my side and pointing it at them. "Wait! Wait Rob! What the hell are you doing!" Myron yelled, sitting his ass back down on the picnic table. "Myron, so you're going to act like you have no idea what I'm talking about?" I asked, as they sat there looking at me like I've lost my mind. "Shelvin, I know Myron is a liar and will lie about any and everything but you're a little more honest than him, so are you going to tell me why you two were molesting my son when he was younger?" I asked, pulling out an individual sleeve that Cornelius picked up for me when I told him I needed a few items, along with the gun. I took out a pair of latex gloves I had in my pocket. I put the sleeve on first and then put the glove on top.

Shelvin started stuttering all over his words. He hasn't done that since we were kids. Myron tried to get up again and walked toward me. "If I have to tell your ass one more damn time, you're going to regret what the hell I'm going to do next," I said. Myron saw that I wasn't playing so he sat back down beside Shelvin. They both were sweating and biting their lips. "Myron, I know the truth so before you insult my intelligence and tell me this never happened. I want to tell you that Ryan emailed his roommate and told him if anything was to happen to him to make sure he gives this to me. Now what I want you two to do is open up the tablet that's on the table and what you're going to do is put in this password, It's "Ryan4Robin6" and watch the first video.

Myron pressed play on the first video and he and Shelvin looked at it as it played out loud. Shelvin had tears in his eyes as he looked up at me. "Rob this still doesn't prove anything," Shelvin said. "I guess you're calling my son a liar huh? Okay, now press the second video after that one," I said. Myron and Shelvin witnessed themselves throwing Ryan in his room and on top of the bed. While Ryan told him he wasn't going to do this with them anymore and how Myron jumped on top of Ryan and started strangling him, and how Shelvin grabbed the pillow and put it over Ryan's face and smothered him with it.

Their mouths dropped when they saw the videos. "Ryan's roommate had cameras in Ryan's room because he knew what kind of lifestyle he was living and he wanted something to protect Ryan in case something was to happen to him. So imagine how I felt when I saw the two people that I grew up with and loved like my brothers, were the ones that molested and killed my son?

Myron you were molesting my son since he was eight years old and Shelvin you started when he was ten. Ryan said it first happened when he spent the night at your house one weekend, when Alexandria and I went out of town for our anniversary and Ryan stayed with you and Diana, along with your children. That was when you took my son's innocence and destroyed his life. How in the hell can you do that to your best friend's son? Someone that loved you and called you his uncle and your wife at the time, his aunt.

Shelvin, how could you do that to my son? Someone who loved you just as well? Ryan said you first did that to him when you took him to the fair that weekend and you acted like you wanted to spend some time with your nephew. How fucking dare you do something so sick to my son.

Now I want you both to tell me it's not true and that Ryan made all this up on you two? Are you going to tell me I'm lying Myron or Shelvin? You're going to tell me that Ryan lied on both of you two and the evidence is right fucking there?" I asked.

Myron dropped his fucking head as well as Shelvin and they both started crying like a little damn baby. "Shelvin, you want to tell me that my son lied on you and that none of this happened?" I asked. "I'm not going to lie Rob and tell you it didn't happen because it did." Shelvin said.

"Well I guess it's nothing else to say Myron and Shelvin. I know you two will never hurt anyone else again in your life because your lives end now," I said, pointing the gun and shooting Shelvin and Myron in the head. I was done talking and hearing all their lies and bullshit because the bottom line is they took my son away from me.

I stood over my former two best friends lifeless bodies, feeling nothing but hate and pure disgust for what they made me do. They destroyed Ryan's life when they started molesting him and they didn't stop there until they killed him as well, so the way I look at it, an eye for an eye and a tooth for a tooth.

I know I'll be held accountable for murdering Myron and Shelvin but no one will ever understand my pain unless they've been in my shoes and they've done what I've done. I'm a father that took justice into my own hands and I don't regret it one bit for what they made me do. "Ryan, I got your justice son," and remember I'm so proud of you and thank you for being a great son. No one can ever judge me until they find themselves where I'm standing and have to get justice for themselves and not waiting for a trial or a judge to sentence them. I sent them straight to hell, where they belong.

CHAPTER 32

"Your Dream"

We all gathered today at the building to cut the ribbon for the grand opening of the "Ryan Jacobs Center." This has been a dream that Ryan told me about and I wanted to honor it in his memory. The children were running around, as if they were excited to be in a new place that was built just for them to enjoy.

We had about ten arcade machines, two pool tables, and air hockey. We had game and movie night for the kids, and for the adults. We also had a dance floor, with a karaoke machine for the entire family to come out. I hired a math tutor to come to the center every Tuesday and Thursday to help the children that are struggling academically in school. I decided to do spoken word, and jazz night for the adults on one side and the children and teens on the other side. I had programs set up for family building and marriage counseling, as well as seminars.

I'm thinking about doing a Career day and have several professional men and women to come in and talk to the children and the youth about the next step in their lives. I even had aerobics and line dancing for the youth as well as the adults. Any and everything you want to do as a family, you could do it at the "Ryan Jacobs' Center."

I walked around the facility, just admiring how I made my son's dream a reality. I bet Ryan is looking down smiling at the dream he had that is now a facility and his name will always be remembered as long as I'm still living. Robin and her best friends jumped in to help and they really made this place what it is. Robin is going to start a big sister and big brother mentoring program with children that don't have any friends or just needed that person in their life that they could talk to outside of their parents.

We want everyone to feel welcome and loved as if the "Ryan Jacobs' Center," is their home and a place for everyone to come together, regardless of race, gender or sexual orientation. Ryan wanted everyone to be able to come together just to show love.

I can't believe it's been six months now since Ryan's murder and the police still haven't found any leads on the case, which I know why that is but they couldn't find any leads on Myron and Shelvin's disappearance either. No one has seen or heard from them in six months. I told the police when they asked me questions that I talked to them that day but haven't seen them at all.

I'm just glad that Cornelius took my cell phone that I put in the mailbox with him so if they were to trace the whereabouts of my phone, they would see that Cornelius and I were together. Cornelius came to the lake and helped me throw the guys in the lake, and we took their cell phones and destroyed them. We threw all the fishing equipment in the lake as well because I knew that after that day, I was never coming back to that lake again.

I went and visited all the people that were on the tapes that Jarod gave me, who Ryan was involved with and asked since I can't change what they did with my son, but would they like to give a generous donation on the center? Some of the guys said "no" but when I showed them their faces in the tapes and how the tape could ruin their lives if it ever was to get out to their precious wives, children and even their jobs, they quickly changed their minds and wrote me out a sizeable check. I got about twenty people from the tapes to write me out a five thousand dollar check towards the center. I told each of them that I've made strict instructions that if anything was to ever happen to me or my daughter to go straight to the tabloids, exposing who they are.

I never had a problem with anyone threatening me or messing with my daughter. I think they all knew I meant business and I wasn't about playing any games with them. Monteiro brought me a check of fifty thousand dollars and he told me to use it well in Ryan's name. I never told Monteiro about me seeing him many times on the tapes but definitely knew all about him. I thanked Monteiro and told him it would definitely be used for good.

I asked Cornelius how he and Jarod were doing because they tried dating each other shortly after Ryan's funeral. Cornelius told me it didn't work because Jarod simply wasn't Ryan and he wasn't ready to date anyone else yet. I told Cornelius that these things were going to take some time and when he's ready to move on and meet someone, he will.

Jarod has been focused on his job and making sure that the facility runs well and that everything is taken care of. He's pretty much devoted his life to the Center and I definitely appreciate everything he's doing around here. Cornelius got a lot more funding from the government and the small business loan to make the "Ryan Jacobs' Center," more competitive and wanted people to come out and support the cause.

Shannon and I are exclusive and she's been helping out a lot around the center. It feels pretty good to be working side by side with her, not just at our main job but with the Center as well. She told me being at the center and helping out just makes her feel like she's giving back to unprivileged children and that's her reward for doing this.

I could see the happiness in her eyes as she talked about the center and she can only imagine how happy my son is about his dream. I told her I'm sure he is and my only regret is I can't run it with him. Shannon told me just because Ryan isn't physically here, he will always be in my heart as well as in this place because this place is what he started and it's going to do really well. I told her I think it will do well too.

Airene and I finally got our divorce and she was sentenced to twelve years in prison, and Ms. Smith and Bradly's mother, Ms. James were sentenced to eight years for their part in the role they played in framing my son. I guess because Airene was the one that planned this entire thing, that's why she got more years than the other two.

I continued looking around, still amazed how beautiful this place is. They really did a great job designing the layout of the center. I couldn't help but smile and thank God that he gave Ryan this vision to help the young people in our community. They now have a place to keep them from doing the wrong thing, by staying away from gangs and getting themselves in trouble. They can help make a difference in someone else's lives to make the world a better place for them. We should never leave anyone behind if we can help them along the way. That's our mission, "A helping hand can go a long way than to let them fall."

I sometimes can't believe that my son is gone and Lord knows I miss Ryan so much, but I believe he's in a better place. I know what I did to Myron and Shelvin will never go unnoticed but no one can blame me because I'm just a father that took justice into my own hands and would do it all over again if I had to. I love you Ryan and may you always look down and smile upon us and your place. The Ryan Jacobs Center is your dream, I just made it come true.

The End,
By John D. McCray